Midnight Voices

Midnight Voices

URBAN FANTASY SHORT STORIES
FROM THE WORLD OF MIDNIGHT
WHISPERS

L.K. Latham

L.K. Latham

Contents

Attack of the Hobgoblin

Danita lifted her long dark hair off her neck and sighed. "Oh, Chiquita. I love this place. So glad you came with me tonight."

Sonya stood as the waitress arrived with another round of drinks. "Me too, Aunty. You were right, I've had my head in the books too long." A beautiful young man with shimmering sunrise skin and bright eyes glided to the table and took Sonya's hand. Sonya giggled and spun with the man onto the crowded dance floor.

Danita smiled and looked up at the countdown clock. Only twenty-one minutes until 2020. "It will be a good year," she whispered to herself.

"We can hope so," the waitress said.

Danita looked up to see her stone-faced old friend, Shirley, place the drinks on the table. "You look too blue for such a party, Shirley."

Shirley sniffed. "Our last party," she said.

Danita took Shirley's hand. "What's this? It's true? I thought it was just a nasty rumor. Sit down, you must tell me."

Shirley shrugged. "Boss says the Phantom's Menace closes its doors for good after last call tonight. Something about expanding the business into other areas. Whatever that means."

Danita downed half her margarita before banging it on the table. "This is wrong. How can he make you work when you will have no work tomorrow? How can we party knowing the doom that waits for us tomorrow?"

Shirley pulled a bar stool close to Danita and sat. "That's the thing," she said. "We still have jobs. He's being very hush-hush about the whole thing. It's so weird. He says no more bar, but we'll still be working for him."

Danita gulped down the rest of her drink. She didn't drink like she used to, and even though Shirley made sure her drinks had less tequila than most, a buzz clouded her thoughts. After staring at her empty glass until her vision cleared, she said, "Look, maybe this will be good, but if not, call me. I just started a new job. I'm Secretary to the President of Communications for the entire University Medical System. I have contacts." She pulled her phone out of the back pocket of her tightest silver pleather pants and tapped the screen. "There, scan."

Shirley reached into her heavy cleavage, squeezed together with a too-tight bustier, and pulled out her phone. She tapped and read her screen. Smiling so much she impressed Danita with her lovely white teeth, Shirley said, "You're a good woman, Danita. Thanks." She twisted to look behind her as though she could hear someone calling her name. "I'd better get back to work. You going to drink the champagne?"

"No," Danita answered, shaking her head. "I've had more than enough. Just a Topo Chico."

Shirley jumped off the stool, adjusted her bustier, and winked. "You got it."

*****

As Shirley walked away, Sonja returned to the table. Her dark hair glistened with gold glitter that was also scattered over her narrow shoulders. Her cheeks were bright pink with excitement, and her round hazel eyes sparkled with delight.

"This is so much fun, Aunty."

Danita laughed. "Not embarrassed to be here with your old aunty, Chiquita?"

"Oh, no!" exclaimed Sonja, slipping off the stool and wrapping her arms around Danita's neck. "You're too much fun. This place is too much fun. It's New Year's Eve. We're going to have a wonderful year."

The beat of the music picked up. The crowd roared with excitement as the twelve-minute mark flashed on all the video screens. Sonja jumped up. "Come on, Aunty! We have to dance in the New Year."

Danita slipped off the stool and stepped onto the dance floor. The music flowed through her, and she shimmied her hips and shoulders to its beat. Sweat trickled down her neck; the coolness it left behind lifted her spirits. The crowd shifted, and she bumped into one of the mirrored columns. Memory stabbed through her stopping her dance.

Was it only in the Fall? The hot night, the beautiful blond boy leaning over her, swinging with her as the music twirled through her head. Such a lovely night, and then there was the gray man with the silver hair and the fancy suit leaning against this very column. She'd danced up to him until fear stole her breath as his beautiful gray eyes ripped through her with hate, loathing, and death.

The crowd shifted, and she flowed away from the column. The music pushed away the nightmare. In the periphery of her vision, she caught sight of a head covered in golden curls. *Could that be the same golden boy?*

She danced her way toward him, but he slid through the crowd toward the exit. As he took the steps leading up to the door, his golden head turned to face the crowd. Such a beautiful boy, but he wasn't her golden boy. This one was small. Cupid lips flashed as pink as his cheeks, complimenting his red silk shirt tucked into beautifully fitting black jeans. For a small man, he filled his pants well.

The young man scanned the crowd, stopping to twinkle a wink at Danita. Beautiful blue eyes danced in the flashing lights of the club. He turned, leaving the bar.

Danita sighed. His loss left an emptiness in her chest she'd forgotten about. Tired of the loud music and sweat, she made her way to the entrance. The manager, Stanley, stood at the door. He stamped her hand and bent over to kiss her cheek. "You're not going to leave me on New Year's Eve, Danita?"

Danita feigned a blush and pushed him away. "You're such a bad *bebe*, Stanley. I'm just going to cool off a minute. I'll be back." She winked at him.

Stanley winked back. "Hurry back. I need a New Year's kiss from my favorite cougar if I'm going to have a good 2020."

*****

The line to get inside the bar wrapped around the building on her left, so Danita turned right, intending to walk just enough to cool off. After one block, she regretted wearing her best stilettos, despite the beautiful curves they formed with her legs. Her ankles ached and her toes demanded freedom. She stopped at the end of the building where it was separated from the next building by an alley. Leaning a hand against the wall, she lifted one leg massaging her ankle and just removed her shoe to wiggle her toes when she heard a deep, guttural, "Argh!"

With a thump and a squish, a man rolled onto the ground in front of her from the alley. Danita, balancing on one foot, froze. Even the tiny bells on the strap stopped ringing. The man in front of her was the most extraordinary man she'd ever seen. He wore a blue suit, so bright it glowed in the streetlights. Gold and red sparkled from his vest. Long shaggy brown hair hung in his face, tangling with a mass of gold rings hanging from each of his ear lobes which stretched below his shirt collar.

Danita put her foot down. The bells rang and and shook her head. His face had a green cast to it. Or was he actually green?

The man pushed himself to his feet. "You loathsome, bloodless, sons of whores and heartless—" He stopped as Danita's foot hit the ground and the bells on her shoe rang. The man straightened his tie before scratching his chin.

Danita stared at the man's face. The green cast disappeared, replaced by a rough, tawny complexion deepened by dark-brown stubble. The man stood almost as tall as Danita, but only because of the red heels on his moss-green boots. Something glittered on the ground between them.

"Oh," she said and bent over to pick up a gold button pressed with an elaborate design. She wished she had her glasses, but even without them, she could see the button was exquisite. Looking up, she saw the empty buttonhole on the man's vest.

"This is yours," she said, holding her hand out to the man.

The man's eyes widened—deep dark eyes that might have looked black if it weren't for the streetlight showering over them, making them glitter with emeralds, moss, and spring leaves. Danita let out a heavy sigh. *I could get lost in those eyes.*

He stepped forward, stretching his hand toward hers but not touching. "Um," he began.

Danita smiled. He was so ugly, she could only call him cute. She winked, smiled, and tossed the button to him. "Here you go."

Faster than lightening, his hand snatched the button in midair. He cleared his throat. "Thank you." His rough voice sounded like gravel rolling down a hill. He opened his mouth to say something else when the crowd on Sixth Street roared.

"Oh no," muttered Danita. "I missed the toast."

"Toast?" asked the man.

Danita put a hand on a hip and scolded, "The New Year's toast. Or don't you know what that is?" She sighed and added, not intending to say it aloud, "And my New Year's kiss. All the beautiful young men dancing and kissing."

"Oh," said the man. "Sorry. Um." He spiraled the button up and down through his fingers, staring at it and then at her and then back to the button.

A loud growl, a thump, and a crack echoed from the alley. The man straightened, gripping the button so tight his knuckles gleamed white. He bit his lip with yellowish, pointed teeth.

Danita stepped forward, half-turning to look into the alley. "Are you all right, *bebe*? Is something happening?"

"Happy New Year," the man said and kissed her.

She had only a moment to react. He looked like the type to slobber a kiss on her cheek, or perhaps he'd let his chapped, thick lips touch hers. But it was a new year, and without a kiss, she'd have no good luck for the year. She'd make it sure it was quick.

But the kiss was nothing like a slobbery peck on the cheek or the shy, passionless passing of lips over lips. When their lips met, the earth shifted.

Thick, dry, chapped lips made their way to hers, but lips of earth, stone, and time touched hers. This was no friendly, innocent, quick peck on the cheek. The kiss lingered. She breathed him in, reminded of springs and summers running through her father's cocoa plantation with cool, black earth between her toes, the rush of tides as she paddled through surf, and the heat of the sun on her skin as she lay naked after a swim in the hidden lagoon.

His body hardened as she pressed into him, wrapping her arms around his massive chest until their bodies, melded by heat, breathed as one. With a final inhale to take in this man's being, Danita stepped away.

She had to take in another breath to clear her lungs of him, already missing him but needing to breathe. "*Feliz Año Nuevo,*" she said. "I should . . ." She pointed to the club. "My niece will wonder where I am."

The man stared at her, saying nothing. She turned to leave. "Wait," he said. "Keep this for me?" He held out his hand to her.

Danita reached out, and he cupped her hand in both of his. They were huge next to hers. He dropped the golden button into her palm.

"Keep it for good luck," he said, then turned and walked into the alley.

The last she knew of him was his voice, low like a boulder rolling down a hill. "You two got this?"

Danita stood there a moment more and then returned to the bar. Stanley, still at the door, motioned her in. Mike stood next to him. They were arm-in-arm, with Mike smiling so wide, Danita couldn't help but grin with him.

"You okay, Danita?" Stanley asked.

"Yes," said Danita. She stood on her toes to give each a kiss on the cheek and say, "*Feliz Año Nuevo, bebe.*"

Her niece and Shirley stood at the table waiting for her.

"Aunty," shouted Sonja. "Where've you been? Did you get your New Year's kiss?"

"Of course she did," said Sonja, winking at Danita. "She's glowing."

"We're going to have a good year," Danita said and toasted them with her glass of Topo Chico.

*****

A mid-sized man in a loud blue suit walked along the quiet street, humming a song no one knew.

A man in a lime-green suit leaned against a streetlight with a burned-out bulb. "Where have you been, friend?" he asked.

The man in the blue suit snorted. "What's the hurry? It's New Year's Day."

The man in the green suit laughed. The rattle of his laughter shook the windows of the houses on the street, but no one noticed.

As his laughter faded, the man in the green suit removed the bowler from his head and bowed to the man in the blue suit. "You, my friend, are indeed a quandary. I think I understand, if I may be so bold in making this proclamation, why it is you were assigned the task at hand."

The man in the blue suit put his hand to his head, and finding no hat, bowed without one. "And if I may make a proclamation equally as bold, if forgiving my bluntness will not offend, Teaser, you are an ass."

Teaser laughed again as he placed his lime-green bowler at a jaunty angle on his head. "I like my new hat. Do you not think it completes my ensemble with the correct seriousness this occasion requires, Mr. Cobalt?"

Cobalt grunted. "There was a jostle," he began as he stretched his neck from side to side. "Two vampires awaiting to pounce an ambush on some traveler of the road, unaware and perhaps fuddled from too much festive expression."

Teaser raised an eyebrow until it pointed like a V over his right eye.

Cobalt nodded. "I dispersed that theory on examination. They were awaiting a particular quarry and were displeased at my interruption of their design."

"Most distressing," said Teaser. "May I compliment you on your recovery. To suffer such an encounter with nothing more lost than a hat and a button is to place you among those listed as memorable in our clan."

"Well." Cobalt snorted. "An interruption in our jostling arose, not entirely without benefit to my new suit. My hat, it is with sadness I must report, took the brunt of the ruffians' disdain. Two werewolves, noble in standing but low in patience for those who hold in contempt the local ordinances against the exchange of hostilities, did refute the black-hearted scoundrels."

Teaser shook his head and sniffled. "The loss of such a button will surely be mourned, but as for the hat, if I may?" Teaser held out his hand as a new bright-blue bowler appeared in it. He offered it to Cobalt.

Cobalt's eyes glowed as he accepted the bowler, holding it with the tips of his fingers as he turned it round and round, pondering every fiber. Finally, he lifted it and placed it on his head at an angle covering his forehead. "I am complete," he said.

Teaser asked, "And your button?"

Cobalt turned away from Teaser. "Not lost," he said. "Where is the house I am to guard?"

Teaser pointed across the street. "The attic is generous and the company varied."

Cobalt nodded. Together, they crossed the street and walked to the back of the building. A motorcycle rounded the corner. Two people got off and parked it in a small garage behind the house.

Teaser pointed to the woman. "The she-wolf makes the offering."

Cobalt scratched his chin and shook his head. "The pair of valiant wolves who negotiated the peace with the hooligans I acquainted myself with at the midnight hour. Interesting to find them in this establishment." He took a step forward. When Teaser didn't follow, he turned to face him. Teaser now stood a head taller than Cobalt.

"A generous attic, you say," said Cobalt.

"With limited headroom," Teaser said with a smile. "The offering is on the doorstep."

Cobalt watched as the pair of wolves in human form entered the house. He wrinkled his nose. "Am I to be paid as a dog by a wolf?"

"Youth," sighed Teaser. "Two young wolves reside within the house. A human woman with a gift retains the house. This retainer is gifted and is our design. The she-wolf provides the portal by which our mutual goals may be achieved."

With each step toward the house, Cobalt decreased in size. Shades of tawny brown and orange and red shifted until his skin shimmered green in the night like the green of the bushes in the darkened yard. He reached the door's stoop and picked up the saucer. He looked at Teaser, who bowed low. Cobalt sipped from the saucer, and Teaser disappeared like a whisper on the breeze. "Contract accepted."

Cobalt listened as the wolves laughed and teased. The front door to the house opened. "Hi," they said in unison to the retainer with the gift. "Didn't expect you for a while," she laughed "I heard you two had an adventure tonight," she replied.

Cobalt slid through the crack between the door and its jamb. "The contract begins."

Tommy's Problem

Louis Tomas Phillip Emanuel St. Genevieve, also known as Tommy, stretched his back, twisting to the right and then to the left. The heartbeats of so many young, fit bodies full of blood and life wrapped him in comfort and satisfaction the likes of which he hadn't felt in over two hundred years. His feet barely touched the street as he bounced off the sidewalk and into the wave of even more bodies weaving up and down Sixth Street on New Year's Eve. Music roared out of bars, keeping time with the rhythm of youth and hope.

He wove through the masses as they celebrated the coming new year until he reached Fifth Street. He turned right and onto the sidewalk. The crowd thinned. He still meandered in crowds walking toward Sixth Street, but now mixed with the gleeful and hopeful were the beggars and thieves holding out hands, picking up cigarette stubs, and stumbling into the unaware.

Tomas turned into an alley next to the Westin Hotel. Checking that the man behind the dumpster was asleep, he stole a last glance around him and disappeared into the shadows. He leaped from windowsill to windowsill until he reached the roof of the hotel.

The lights of the pool danced along the wall of the cabana and the doors to the elevators. Music from Sixth Street floated up and over the building along with the whispered roar of people waiting with the impatience that only humans can have for another year to check off on their calendars.

With a leap, he jumped to the ledge where Max squatted, watching the city as though it might vanish.

"I like it up here," Tomas said. "I can take in all the life."

Max turned his face to meet Tomas. For a moment, the dancing lights of the pool reflected gold and green in the depths of his eyes, dark and clear like time. He raised the side of his mouth in a smirk. "I don't understand the need to glorify a date. You're late."

Tomas laughed. "Can't goad me tonight, old man. I'm in too good a mood and in my new, lucky shirt." He sat on the ledge, letting his feet dangle against the wall as he adjusted the cuffs of the red silk sleeves.

Max returned his gaze to the street below. "Cesar told you about the virus spreading in China." He pointed to the people below him. "They'd do better to shelter now."

"The youth will always celebrate life," Tomas said. "It's their nature. They will celebrate even when death walks among them. Give them tonight."

The first chords of the countdown drifted over them. They listened.

Tomas sighed. "You didn't ask me here to talk about the virus. What's wrong?"

Max stood and looked down at Tomas. "You have a problem," he said. "Unfinished business."

Tomas rose, narrowing his eyes and tensing his shoulders. His toes curled, ready to pounce, but Max pointed below them.

"Richard's in town and looking for you," said Max.

Tomas turned his gaze to where Max pointed. "Damn him! What does he want?" He didn't realize he'd said it out loud until Max answered.

"Revenge?"

Tomas watched as Max's usual straight, stern face lifted with a smile as fireworks lit the sky, turning his pale face red, and his long, sharp white teeth glistened gold. Tomas returned the grin. "We're inside the city," he said. "Could be complicated."

Max nodded, his own eyebrows raising. "Richard brought friends with him and didn't ask Cesar's permission." He stretched his arms before him and cracked his knuckles. "We have his blessing to deal with all of them."

Tomas laughed. "We're going to do this together? People will think you like me."

Max shook his head and rolled his shoulders. "Clay's waiting for our call to clean up. Enough talk." Max stepped off the ledge, dropping the twenty floors to the shadows along the street's edge.

Still laughing, Tomas followed.

*****

Tomas stood in the shadows of the rooftop bar watching old allies on the street below. Roman, lean, fit, and snarling slouched against the corner of the bank building. His white arms and chest glowed beneath his black leather vest. Silver chains hung around his neck, and his long silver hair almost disappeared as he leaned away from the streetlight. He smoked a cigarette, blowing the smoke slowly and deliberately into the crowd. The crowd only noticed him when the smoke mixed with their own. His eyes, like black darts, cut through the smoke, searching. No one smiled at him, even after the countdown and celebration welcoming 2020 began.

Richard stood next to him, his arms folded over his chest, watching. His gray silk suit gleamed in the streetlights, turning red, green, and gold in the glare of the fireworks. Thick blond hair, smoothed back to a neat curl at his neck, and a thin blond beard gave him a President of the Board look, but his clear blue eyes held so much anger, they could tear through the souls of those unfortunate enough to look at him.

Across the street stood two more. With their jeans, leather jackets, and dark hair, they blended into the college crowd. They took turns walking first a block north and then a block south, searching the crowd. They returned, looked at Richard, and shook their heads. Richard didn't acknowledge them, only pinched his lips tighter and narrowed his eyes more.

Tomas shook his head. "I've been standing here for a quarter of an hour. I'd forgotten how thick Richard is. Oh, Roman's here too.

Remember him?" He turned to look at Max, sitting at the table and tapping his phone. "Is this really the time to check your status?"

Max's phone beeped. He tapped it again and stood, then put it in his back pocket. "Not so thick. He brought two more. They're three blocks over. The Eugenes will deal with them. I don't know Roman."

Tomas nodded. "That's right. He didn't go to Galveston with me."

Max lifted one corner of his mouth in a sneer. "Then he's smarter than you."

Tomas shrugged. "Whatever. Odd, him being with Richard. Never really liked him."

"And he has good taste." Max stood next to Tomas. "Are we going to do this, or do you intend to reminisce all night?"

Tomas burst into laughter. His tinkling laugh wove its way through the bar patrons. They laughed with him, feeling the joy of the night. The sound spread across the bar, falling into the crowd on the street. "Always to the point, old man. But you're right. I suppose, as it's my fight, you'll be hanging in the shadows in case he kills me?"

"Yes," Max said.

Still laughing, Tomas put his hand on Max's shoulder. "You do nothing half-assed, and Richard likes a show. It's going to be a fun night."

Tomas looked down and across the street. Laughter continued to float across the mass of celebrants. Richard looked up. His arms dropped, and his hands clenched into fists so tight Tomas could see the whitening of his knuckles. Those in the crowd near him shook with fear, which turned to rage. Unsure why they were afraid and angry, they gulped from the cups and bottles in their hands, ducked their heads, and pushed the crowd forward until the bare emotions left them. Those who couldn't move far enough away clutched their own fists and punched, not knowing why they hated the face in front of them.

Tomas smiled the beautiful, cherubic grin that won over the hearts of the most bitter, the most lonely, the most amorous of his adversaries. Richard's anger grew. From the crowd, insults were shouted. Fists hit flesh. Blood spurted from a broken nose. More punches, more blood, more insults, and then a bang echoed across Sixth Street. Screams and yells followed as sirens broke over them.

"Well, old man," said Tomas. He didn't look at Max. Max had already faded into the shadows behind him, out of sight. "It's started."

He stepped as close to the edge of the patio as he could get, unseen by anyone who looked up. People ran up and down the street except for Richard. He remained standing, waiting. His three companions stood behind him. Four pairs of eyes glared at Tomas, their hate fueling the fire burning in the crowd.

Tomas dropped his grin and nodded once to Richard and his old friends, motioning them to the side street.

*****

Sirens filled the air, but music continued to pour out of the bars. Red and blue lights flashed. Yellow ambulances on the side street waited, lights flashing, for the all-clear from the police. Tomas strode past the lights and sounds two blocks north of Sixth Street. People continued to stream to the street party, but now it mingled with a steady stream of bodies moving away from the party.

He walked another block, looked around him, and turned into an alley. Richard stood in the middle of the dead-end alley.

"Did you think you could get away with it, Tomas?" asked Richard. His voice, deep and harsh, did not hide his hatred.

"So formal, Dick? You always called me Tommy." Tomas scanned the alley. "Surprised to find you still walking about. Without Leonard to protect you, I was sure you'd wake up with a stake in your heart by now."

Richard's shoulders shook. His mouth tightened even as words forced their way out. "You killed Leonard—the one vamp who gave us the strength to defeat the Eldests, the one chance we had to live the lives meant for us. He gave us everything, gave you even more, and you betrayed him. You betrayed us."

"You're such a cliché, Dick," said Tomas. He took a step forward, tilting his head to the side, listening as Richard's friends scuffed their feet on the ground, smiling as the silver chains on Roman's neck clanked against his skin. He inched closer to Richard with each step. "Can't even come to a fight without an army of goons too scared to know how to fight well. And that suit! Leonard wore it with style. He carried the look like a vamp should." Tomas stood in front of Richard now. He straightened his back to his full height, but Richard still looked down at his face, staring into Tomas's eyes. "You still look like an angry, little nibbler with no balls to stand up for yourself."

Richard roared and pushed his right arm forward as a silver dagger slipped from his sleeve. Tomas twisted, grabbing Richard's arm, and squeezed until Richard dropped the dagger. A fist hammered Tomas's side, and he flew into a wall. Tomas stood and shook his shoulders to loosen his muscles. "Roman, you finally learned to throw a decent punch."

Other hands grabbed for him. He ducked the first pair of hands only to feel a boot kick his knees from under him. He pushed himself up even as a pair of hands grabbed his shoulders, pulling him to his feet.

Roman grabbed Tomas's hair. "Learned a lot while you were away," he spat and swung his fist into Tomas's jaw.

A crack echoed in Tomas's ears. He threw his own fist into Roman's face, allowing himself a moment of satisfaction as he heard another loud crack.

"Grab hold of him!" shouted Richard.

Tomas's fist swung, pounding into the side of a dark head. He kicked and grinned as his foot broke bone. Someone kicked the back of his legs. He fell, hitting his head on the concrete edge of a wall, and his vision went dark. It lasted only a moment, but it was the moment his opponents waited for. Two pairs of hands held him up, pushing his back into a wall. His vision returned.

Richard glared down into his face, spitting his words. "Lost your wit, have you, Tomas? I've been waiting for this for a long time." Richard lifted his hand. The silver in the dagger flickered in the streetlights as he pushed the sharp edge into Tomas's throat.

The force of Roman's hand on his shoulder loosened just enough for Tomas to feel the shift.

Tomas laughed.

Richard's determination faltered even as a trickle of blood ran over the knife's edge. "Can't even die without a smirk, can you? You stupid, ungrateful brat!"

Tomas struggled but forced his jaw to move. "Who's the stupid one, Richard? You should have done better surveillance. I have new friends now."

The streetlights dimmed. Richard turned. At the end of the alley stood Max, his feet apart, knees bent, and eyes burning as they stared at Richard.

Richard looked at Max, back to Tomas, and back to Max. "This isn't your fight! I've got no argument with you, old man," Richard yelled. "And you've got no rights over us."

Max stepped farther into the alley. "Not your city," he said. His mellow, smooth voice floated over the air toward Richard and the others. A chill descended in the alley. "I give you one chance to withdraw, now, untouched. Clay?"

Clay stepped into the alley. He removed his top hat. "I'm ready to clean up, whoever loses. Funerals for those who die well."

Roman's grip on Tommy's shoulder tightened, even as he muttered so only Tomas could hear, "I didn't want this."

"Stand your ground," Richard said through clenched teeth. "Clay won't fight. We took Tomas. We'll take the other old man. Call the others."

Two figures jumped into the alley from the lowest roof. Richard and his men stood between Max and the newcomers.

"Werewolves," spat Richard. "You ally yourself with werewolves, Tomas? You've become even more pathetic."

"Have you met the Eugenes?" Tomas said. "They live in this city, too. Everything okay, Eugenes?"

"We're good," a male voice answered with the slightest of growl in his throat.

"Can we get this over with?" a female voice added, the growl in her voice more pronounced than her brother's. She held a thick board. Nails sticking out of one end dripped with red. "The clubs are still open."

"That's why you're my best girl, sweetie." Tomas tried to laugh, but his jaw refused to open. He managed a good snicker.

"Traitor!" shouted Richard. He lifted the dagger and swung it to slice Tomas's throat.

A howl like a roar filled the alley. Max grabbed Richard's arm before his swing passed its zenith. He ripped Richard's arm out of its socket and struck the man behind Richard with the hand that still held the knife. The knife fell to the grown with a sweet ting. The Eugenes swung clubs into the heads of those holding Tomas. Tomas fell to the ground in a mound of beaten and bloody flesh. He shook his head and pushed himself to his hands and knees.

He looked up to see Richard staring at him, hate oozing from his eyes and essence. The silver knife lay near Tomas's hand. He picked it up. Richard pushed his remaining arm beneath him, but blood poured from the open socket on the other side, and he could only turn away from Tomas.

Max bit into the neck of his opponent and broke his back with a loud crack. Roman rolled on the ground and remained there, holding his head as he crouched beneath the male Eugene, one hand raised in supplication as he pressed the other hand to his neck to slow the blood pumping out of a small hole.

Tomas pushed himself to his feet picking up the knife in his right hand. He leaned over, grabbing Richard's bearded chin with his left hand. "Should have left while you could, old *friend*." He raised his arm and sliced Richard's neck with a long, quick slice, then tugged Richard's head the rest of the way off his shoulders.

"You took your time getting here," Tomas said, dropping Richard's head to the ground. He pushed on his jaw with one hand. It wouldn't move. "Do you mind?"

"You looked so confident walking in," Max said, lifting the corners of his mouth into a devil's grin. He grabbed Tomas's jaw with both hands and pushed it into place with a deafening crack. "I thought you wanted a bit of fun first."

Tomas harrumphed. "Ow," he muttered and turned to the werewolves standing over their conquests. Each so tall and thin, each so confident as humans, so graceful as wolves. They would be devastating foes. Keeping his hand on his chin to keep it in place, he bowed. "Thank you."

"We done?" the Eugenes said as one.

Clay walked into the alley. "It's time you departed," he said. "Shall I deal with the live one too?"

Roman whimpered. "I yield. I yield."

The Eugene sister pounded her nail-encrusted board in her hand. "I gave you that shirt, Tommy."

Tomas looked down. "I loved this shirt," he moaned. "I'm sorry, sweetie."

"Right," she said. "See if I get you anything nice again."

The Eugenes leaped onto the roof of the small building at the end of the alley and disappeared, but even as they left, their muttering trickled into the ally.

"Way too easy."

"Not much of a fight if we don't even get out the wolf."

"Can't believe he ruined the shirt I gave him for Christmas."

Despite the pain in his jaw, Tomas laughed. "See you later, sweetie."

Max stood over Roman. "Fight's out of this one. You'll stay in Austin where I can watch you. Adjust or die. Those are your choices."

Tomas gave Clay the dagger. He tugged at his shirt. "My favorite shirt. She's not going to let me live this one down. You good, Roman?"

Roman looked up, snarling. "Whatever."

"Your usual cheerful self," Tomas said. "You'll like Austin. I do, for now."

Max followed Tomas to the street. Behind them, the alley turned from dark to black as shadows enveloped the opening until it merged into nothing a human would see. A paramedic on the corner, treating those with cuts and bruises from the street fight, rushed toward Tomas with his medical box. "Let me take a look at you."

Max stood in front of him. "He's fine. You should see the other guy."

The paramedic stared for a moment before returning to his station on the corner. A moment later, he forgot about the blond-haired kid with the torn and bloodied shirt.

"There'll be more. You sure you want your friend to stay here?" Max asked as he and Tomas walked unseen down the street. Police on horseback moved through the crowd, disrupting the last of the street-fighters. Revelers, intending to party as long as they could, moved as far away as they could from the combatants and those who looked like combatants.

Tomas shrugged his shoulders. "You don't change sides and not make enemies. Roman's a good guy. He didn't want to be here tonight. Besides, better to keep him close. He's smart, too young to know what he his, but smart enough to become a threat."

"Did you change sides?" Max stopped walking to peer down at Tomas's face.

Tomas pulled his hand through his golden curls, then stopped and shook his hand to knock off the dried blood. They stood outside the Phantom's Menace. The line to enter still wrapped around the corner. Stanley, the manager, motioned them to the side door. Both wore shirts torn and covered with blood. Tomas realized Max was covered in as much blood as he was, only it camouflaged better with his black T-shirt.

They closed the door behind them, walking along the dark, narrow hallway to the private elevator leading to Cesar's office. "I suppose I never believed in Leonard's idea of a perfect world," said Tomas. "Ruling is fun, but . . ." Tomas trailed off as the elevator opened.

"Max! Tommy!" shouted both CC and Cesar as they jumped off the couch and ran to them. "What the hell happened to you?"

Tomas grinned, taking the clean towel from CC's hands. "It's good to have friends."

Finding Mr. Doodles

"So, that's where he's been," said Officer Charles LaRoux. He stood and tugged on his belt to refit it over his bulging middle.

Detective Richard Harris remained squatting next to the body of the young man who'd washed up on the edge of the Seawall. He scratched his chin before standing up to tower over the patrolman the Chief, his new boss, had assigned to drive him around while he "got the feel of the place." That was two weeks ago, and the patrolman still showed up every day to drive him wherever he needed to go.

Harris sighed and looked over the heads of LaRoux and the forensics team as the sun dipped its toes into the waters of the Gulf of Mexico. He would have enjoyed just standing and watching the sunset, but the noise of the Pleasure Pier roared in his ears. After a career in the Army as a Master Sergeant, he didn't need to shout to make himself heard. "Are you going to tell us who he is?"

LaRoux grinned, showing off full white teeth. "Sure." His dark eyes glinted in the golden sun. "Ronny Dohl, that young *arteest* who took one of those the new houses over on 25th Street there by Ms. DuMond's. You know—she's the one with that damned cat everyone's always complaining about. I swear, one of these days me and that cat are going to go at it. It's gonna be me or him. Vicious little shit. Why, just the other night, I got my usual call to go down there—"

Harris interrupted LaRoux without looking up from his phone where he searched city records for a Ronny Dohl. "Does the cat have anything to do with Mr. Dohl here?"

Officer LaRoux lifted his finger to Harris. "You hit it right on the money there, detective." He giggled a deep almost laugh but not quite snort that made his belly jiggle. "That's why you're the detective. Always thinking. My wife, now she's always on to me for being a patrolman. Says I should be a detective by now, but I got no mind to do that. Nope, there's nothing like riding round town talking to folks, making them feel safe just by waving out my window and saying hey. Detective shows up, and right away everyone knows something bad's happened. Don't want to be known for that. You know, if it hadn't been for Ms. DuMond and that shit of a cat, we might never've been out looking for Ronny Dohl."

Harris lifted his gaze from his phone. "Warrant out for him. Animal cruelty, and he's got an eviction order placed two weeks ago. He hasn't been in the water that long. Where's he been hiding?"

"He hadn't left the house. Ms. DuMond, for all her hollerin', is an old softy when it comes to pretty boys. Then again." LaRoux stopped, puckered his lips and eyebrows. Harris opened his mouth to ask a question when LaRoux added, "She didn't take too kindly at all to him kicking her cat. You have to admit, it's pretty low to kick a cat."

Harris folded his arms over his chest, let out a long breath, and asked, "When did he kick her cat?"

"Two nights ago. That's when she made the official complaint."

Harris looked down at the technicians zipping the body bag closed. The older of the two looked up at him, nodding. "I'd say no more than two days in the water, but that's unofficial."

"Well, seems like we'll have to—"

"Oh, no detective," moaned LaRoux.

Harris shook his head as LaRoux's pasty white face grimaced. "You're supposed to drive me around to meet everyone. Time to meet Ms. DuMond."

*****

"Don't you 'Ms. DuMond' me, Charlie LaRoux," shouted Ms. Du-Mond from her porch overlooking 25th Street. Like the other houses on the street, the house stood on stilts with neat stairs shooting up to a porch lined with gingerbread and hanging plants. Ms. DuMond's house gleamed pink, white, and gold in the streetlights. Two elaborate pots containing red, red roses stood on either side of her front door, while small pots with miniature roses lined the steps leading up to her patio.

In front of her hissed the largest, ugliest cat Detective Harris had ever seen. Two gold disks glared at Harris from behind filthy, bushy gray eyebrows that almost hid its eyes. Beneath a stubby gray nose, a thick gray mustache-like fur hung over yellow teeth gleaming in the porch light like the porticos of Hell. And it was huge. Standing on all fours, with its back rounded like a hump, it stood almost up to Ms. DuMond's knees.

Ms. DuMond, in comparison, looked even more frightening, even though she stood taller than no one's shoulders. Golden eyes danced with excitement even as she narrowed her eyes and curled her lips in contempt.

"I told you that man weren't up to no good," she continued to yell at LaRoux. "But did you listen to me? No, you have to wave me off like I'm just nobody's old grandma, too crazy to know what she's doing. Partying all night like no good Christian ever walked this town. Leaving trash all bout that place. And calling himself an artist. Artist my eye! No good artist was ever as mean as that man to my cat. Just look at him. He's still traumatized. See how's he shaking?"

The only shaking Harris saw was in Officer LaRoux as he raised his hands. "Now, Ms. DuMond, you know I take everything you tell me to heart. Didn't I help you file that eviction form? Didn't I file that animal cruelty charge? I done everything what the law—"

"The law!" shouted Ms. DuMond. The cat stepped aside. Harris noticed it limped on one of its hind legs. Ms. DuMond picked up the cat and wrapped her arms around it, squeezing it to her chest. "I have half a mind to send you the vet bill for all the good you and your law did. Just look at his tail. Anyone can—"

LaRoux took advantage of Ms. DuMond stopping to turn her cat around to say, "I brought you our newest and best detective on the force, Ms. DuMond."

Ms. DuMond turned her gaze to Harris. One eyebrow rose in a

tall, spiked point. Harris watched as the cat's face mirrored its owner. "Detective?"

"Detective Harris, ma'am. Officer LaRoux told me what kind of tenant and neighbor Mr. Dohl was to you. I'm amazed at how you kept your temper as long as you did."

Ms. DuMond's face relaxed, but her icy gaze didn't leave Harris's face. "Told you *all* about him, did he?"

LaRoux's fingers rubbed at his color. "All 'bout the parties and him kicking poor Mr. Doodles there almost to death."

"Mr. Doodles?" asked Harris.

"The cat, detective," answered LaRoux.

Harris looked back at Ms. DuMond. Her eyes shot into his for a moment, but then she turned and sat on the rocking chair. Mr. Doodles in her lap almost hid her face. "That was the last straw," she said, loud enough to be heard. "What kind of man kicks a poor little kitty? Not a good man, that's for sure."

"Not a good man at all, ma'am," replied Harris, taking one step through the gate into the small patch of garden. He looked around, breathing in the exquisite aroma of roses. They filled the small patch of front yard. Red, white, yellow, and pink roses burst through layers of dark and light greens even in the glare of the streetlights and over-large security light sticking out from the roof of the house. "Beautiful garden," he said, unable to help himself.

"You're Libby Harris's husband, aren't you?" asked Ms. DuMond.

"Yes, ma'am," Harris froze and studied the face of Ms. DuMond, but it was the sneer on Mr. Doodles's face that caught his attention.

Ms. DuMond continued, "Fine woman. Met her at church last Sunday." She narrowed her eyes again. "Haven't seen you there?"

Harris cleared his throat, but LaRoux answered. "Been working. Both of us. He's got a lot to learn about the place."

Ms. DuMond nodded. "Sure, but I expect to you see there soon. You too, Charlie. Your poor mamma's worried you're working too much. Don't know why? With that girth on you, nobody's running you down."

Harris tried and failed to hide a grin.

"And as for you," Ms. DuMond returned her gaze to Harris, "your wife said she'd like to grow roses. I got a few cuttings all ready for her. You take them to her for me."

Harris nodded. "Thank you. I will. However, as long as I'm here, I'd like to talk to you about Mr. Dohl."

Mr. Doodles hissed and jumped off Ms. DuMond's lap and ran down the stairs, still hobbling to favor his right rear leg. Harris had just enough time to lift a leg to avoid the cat when the gate slammed shut. Mr. Doodles leaped onto the gate post and hissed once more at Harris before leaping onto the sidewalk to run/hobble down the street.

LaRoux threw up his hands just as Ms. DuMond stood and put her hands on her hips. At the same time, they yelled to Harris, "Now, what 'cha go and upset Mr. Doodles for?"

*****

Harris parked the car and read the text again. *Accidental Drowning. Sure?* He'd texted back.

Yes.

Harris scratched his chin and shook his head. "No way," he muttered as he got out of the car. "Those scratches could have been the cats, but—"

He stopped mid-thought as a chill ran up his spine. He looked around. The parking lot for the medical examiner's building was empty. A few stars poked through the city lights as wispy clouds glided the airwaves toward the mainland. A hearse pulled in and circled to the back of the building. The only sounds were the cars on Broadway and just beneath them, the ever-present moan of waves trying and failing to conquer the shore.

He tossed his cap into the car, pulled out his backpack, and went into the building. The whisk of the door closing echoed in the empty hall. He'd been in the building once with Officer LaRoux and remembered the directions to the exam room. While the lights were dim, it was easy to see. He smiled at the sound of his footsteps marching through the hall. Of all the things he missed about Army life, it was the sounds he missed most. Reveille in the mornings, the quick snap of heels on linoleum when the Colonel entered the room, the steady crunch of boots on gravel as he led recruits on long marches through the hills.

A door at the end of the hall opened. Bright light covered a bulky man in scrubs and a long apron standing at the door. "That you, Detective Harris?"

"Yes," replied Harris. "Dr. Tanner?"

Dr. Tanner didn't smile. "Come on in and see for yourself, but it won't change the facts."

Harris forced a smile on his lips. "I appreciate you staying late to help with this."

Dr. Tanner shrugged as he pulled a gurney into the center of the room and uncovered the body of Ronny Dohl. "Every time we get a new detective, he thinks he knows more than science. Dohl's alcohol level was 3.8. I found abrasions on his ankles, knees, and hands. He fell. He hit his head on some rocks and drowned."

Harris nodded and pointed to the scratches covering most of the torso and limbs. "And these?"

Dr. Tanner put a hand on his hip. He rolled his eyes. "Cats."

Harris lifted his hand to scratch his chin but stopped. "Cats or a cat?"

"Detective," sighed Dr. Tanner. "You've been to the Seawall. It's filled with feral cats. They also took a few bites. You'll get used to it."

Harris opened his mouth, but Dr. Tanner raised his hands. "Look, I'm sorry, detective. Had a bad day, and I'm taking it out on you. Let me start again." He offered a hand to Harris. "Call me Mel."

Harris shook hands with the doctor. "Richard or Harris will do."

"Well, Richard," Dr. Tanner leaned against a table, "Ronny Dohl here isn't unusual. He'd been drinking heavily. Nothing else in his blood. The cats living in the Seawall are just about back to their numbers pre-Ike. There's really nothing unusual here."

"I believe you, Mel. I just want to know all I need to know."

"By the way," Dr. Tanner asked, re-covering the body. "Where's LaRoux? Thought he was your shadow."

Harris laughed. "Still searching for Ms. DuMond's cat. Your text saved me from being out there searching for that damned thing. You ever seen such an ugly cat?"

Dr. Tanner laughed. "Everyone knows Ms. DuMond's cat."

The door opened, and a voice like gravel loomed into the room. "Body ready, Dr. Tanner?"

Dr. Tanner looked back at Harris. "You done?"

Harris nodded, and a short man, broader than Harris, limped in. Thick, knotted black and gray hair covered a fat round head that sat on shoulders broader even than Harris's. Harris froze, watching as the man had to turn sideways to fit through the door. Long tannish gray fingers gripped the edge of the gurney and pulled it toward the door. The man turned to push it out the door. Before closing the door, he looked at Harris. Bright gold dots shone through bushy gray-black eyebrows that half hid his eyes. The eyebrows were thin compared to the thick, dirty gray of the mustache concealing the man's mouth, except that as he left, the man must have grinned, for his bottom lip opened into a cup, and pointed yellow teeth glared in the bright exam-room lights.

"Catch you around, detective," the voice, like rocks, said.

*****

Harris drove down 25th Street and found Officer LaRoux sitting on Ms. DuMond's porch. The two of them sat on rocking chairs, drinking from tall glasses.

As he got out of the car, Ms. DuMond shouted to him, "You find Mr. Doodles?"

Before he could answer, LaRoux answered her. "Now, you know he always turns up when he's good and ready to. Want some iced tea, detective?"

"He doesn't have time to sit around and chew the fat with you, Charlie LaRoux. The man actually works, and he's got a bride waiting at home for him."

"Ms. DuMond, they been married six months. I'd hardly call them bride and groom anymore. In fact—"

"Just 'cause you ain't got any romance in you doesn't mean the detective don't. Why just look at him. He's itching to get away."

Harris watched as the two stopped talking to stare at him. He'd never felt embarrassed about anything, by anyone, at any point in his life, but as he stood there, heat rushed to his face and he opened his mouth to answer but could find no words.

"Don't suppose you need me driving you about anymore, do you?" asked LaRoux.

"Never did," answered Ms. DuMond. "Anyone can see the man knows what's what."

"Thank you, Officer LaRoux, but I think I've got it from here."

LaRoux stood. "Then I'm on my way home. Good night, Ms. DuMond. You take care now." As he walked down the stairs, he waved Harris away. "Don't fret on me, detective. I'm just around the corner. Good night."

"Come up here, detective," said Ms. DuMond. "I've got those cuttings ready for your wife."

Harris drove up 25th Street to the Seawall and parked next to the fishing pier. The smell of the rose cuttings filled his car with their sweet scent, and for a moment, he forgot he was still working. As he stepped out of the car, he breathed in the fresh air filled with salt and fish. Leaning against the car, he waited. An old jeep pulled up behind him, and a man got out of the car with his fishing gear and walked to Harris.

"How's it going, Harris?"

Harris grinned. "John," he said and laughed. "You know, it doesn't get easier. Still want to call you colonel." He sighed and fell in to walk next to his old friend. "It's been one of those days you said I'd have if I came to Galveston."

John nodded. "Figured as much by your phone call. Want you to meet someone."

"Galveston's been good to you. Don't know I ever saw you so relaxed." Harris couldn't get over the transformation in the rigid, so formal officer he'd served with for so long as he shrugged and walked, not marched, to the end of the fishing pier.

"Give it time. You'll get used to Island Time."

A row of cats sat along one side of the pier. Others ran up and down the pier, peeking into pails and baskets. Most of the cats watched the two men move to the end of the pier. One cat, larger than the others, sat on a post in the far corner. He kept his back to them, still, as though waiting.

"Got that rod fixed, Doodles," John said.

The large cat jumped off the post and stood on his two back legs. Long fingers reached forward, taking the offered fishing rod. "Damn stupid way to catch fish," its voice, like gravel on a dirt road, answered.

John guffawed. "You'd rather jump in the water to catch them?"

Doodles spit. "I'd drown. You know we don't take to water. Will drown every time we touch it. I hate it."

John leaned against the rail. "What don't you hate?"

The man/cat said nothing.

"I suppose you have a good story for how Dohl ended up in the water."

"Accident," coughed the man/cat.

John shook his head. "No such thing with the two of you. You should have come to me when Dohl fell in, Doodles. Now my friend here has to clean up your mess."

Doodles turned around and looked up at Harris's face. "Accidental drowning. What's to clean up? I picked him up and woke him up, didn't I?"

Harris studied the face that stretched to look up into his face. It had the same gold beads flickering and reflecting light from behind the same filthy, thick gray eyebrows as Mr. Doodles. Yellow teeth glistened from behind the same long, furry, gray mustache as Mr. Doodles. And it had the same voice, like rocks falling down a hill, that had spoken to him in the medical examiner's office. The only difference was a long, pointed nose sticking out between the eyes and mustache. Gray-green skin shimmered from the fog blowing in.

"How many faces you got?" Harris asked.

"Doodles," exclaimed John as he leaned over the short man. "Give the man a break. One face. What have I told you about that?"

"You said he could handle it," snapped Doodles.

"Gnomes," said John. "Sneaky bunch. This one, more so than most."

"It keeps me alive." Doodles swung the fishing rod back and forth. "Feels good. Thanks for fixing it."

"And Dohl?" Harris asked John.

"My brother," said Doodles. "The two-faced, piss-ant, son of a-."

John pointed to a basket next to his feet. Harris reached down and opened the lid. Green eyes like demon lights flashed up at him from a tiny cat-like face with long, pointed ears.

"Let me out of here," the tiny cat-like thing shouted.

"Nope," said John, closing the lid. "I warned you two what would happen if you two couldn't keep the peace."

Harris watched as Doodles lowered the fishing rod and drooped his head. "You're not going to throw him in the drink, are you?"

"You're the one that should be thrown in the drink, Doodles." John shook his head. "Harris, sometimes it's like herding—well." He looked around him. "Cats. Damned frustrating. These two have lived and died on the island for over a hundred years. They know all the haunts and help keep folks from getting carried away. Now," he shook his head again, "Ronny Dohl is dead, and no one can see him again. He's got to go."

Doodles's shoulders slumped more. Harris thought he heard a sniff. "Guess you're right."

"Hey!" squealed the tiny pebble voice from the basket. "Don't I get a say in this?"

Harris and John both said, "No."

"Sorry, bro," Doodles said. "If Ms. DuMond didn't need me so much, I'd go with you. Unless the colonel's going to put you back in the water."

John handed the basket to Harris. "You wanted to be here. Here you go."

"What am I supposed to do with him?"

"Keep him away from Doodles."

"What!" shouted the little voice. The lid to the basket popped up, and the tiny gray-green cat-like head shot out. "You're sending me to live with this palooka? No way! Let me out of here. I'll find an attic to live in. Somewhere far away. Last thing I need—"

Harris slammed the lid down on the basket. "John, my lady love won't take kindly to a gnome in the yard."

"What? A kitten? She'll love it. You got the rose cuttings from Ms. DuMond?"

Harris nodded.

John held out his hand, and Harris pulled cuttings from his backpack. John pushed the cuttings into the basket.

"Ow!" shouted the creature. "One scratch would do."

"Plant these when you get home. Some in the yard, some in pots. The roses will bind him to your property until the next hurricane comes and kills the roses. That's why Ms. DuMond keeps so many roses in the yard and pots on the porch."

"That's not fair!" shouted the little voice.

"It's that or back in the Gulf, and you can hope you wash up somewhere comfortable." John turned to Doodles. "As for you . . ."

Doodles stood up straight. "I was within my rights to defend myself. Besides, I did't push him in. He was drunk and fell in."

John nodded. "After you slugged him. One more infraction, and I'm taking the lawnmower to Ms. DuMond's yard."

"You wouldn't dare." Doodles glared at him.

John smirked. "You've got it good there. It'd be a shame if you had to move."

Harris watched as Doodles took a step away from John and pouted.

"Speaking of Ms. DuMond," Harris said. "She's worried about you."

"I'm going, I'm going," muttered Doodles. "See you 'round Dohl."

"Later, bro," called back the voice in the basket.

Harris nodded his head as Doodles dropped to four paws and ran off the pier and down the street. "My lady love will approve of a soft, cuddly kitten."

Harris put the basket with the kitten in his car. "And that's all she better see of you, Dohl. When you said there was more to Galveston than vampires, I didn't know this is what you meant."

John laughed. "There's more than what you see around here. Just keep your eyes open. Glad you wanted to come. It's a lot of work keeping order around here. I've needed someone other than LaRoux."

"LaRoux?"

"Why do you think he's been tagging along with you all this time? Knows every haunt and demon in town. He's almost as good a resource as Dohl."

"I'm a hell of a lot better than that oaf!" shouted Dohl's voice from the car.

Harris filled his lungs with the soft, wet air blowing in from the Gulf. "I'm going to like it here."

Before the First Bite

Luna sat on the bench hidden under the stairs between the original Goddess of Justice statue and the remains of the ship *La Belle*. Kicking off her new shoes, she pulled her right foot across her lap to massage her toes and sucked in her breath to not yell when her fingers hit the blister on the ball of foot. Wrinkling her nose, she whispered, "Ow! Ow! Ow!"

She set her sore foot on the icy floor and looked at her new shoes. The bling, the three-inch spikes, the black-gold chain, and the sparkling red heart-shaped padlocks twinkled in the floor lights, reminding her why she'd worn the shoes. They were beautiful. Mama said they weren't practical for leading tours in the museum, but what did she know about fashion, curvaceous legs, or a tantalizing butt?

Luna set the shoes next to her on the bench. "I'm not my mama."

A series of dongs poured out of the museum's speakers, filling the air with a hesitant melody, followed by Francine's voice. "Ladies and Gentlemen, the museum will close in fifteen minutes. We invite you to visit us again . . ."

Leaning her back against the cool marble wall, Luna unfocused her eyes to wait for closing. A man and a woman stood arm-in-arm, looking at the ship from the opposite side of the room. The man pointed to something inside the ship, and Luna listed as the woman whispered something. They laughed.

"Keep moving," Luna said under her breath. "Don't ask questions. Just move along."

Luna pulled out her phone. Fourteen minutes left. She didn't want to put her shoes back on or talk to anybody. She hated answering the same questions day in and day out. Working at the museum had been Mama's idea. "It'll be fun," she'd said. "You'll learn something," she'd said. "And it will give you money to buy some new clothes." The summer was only half over, and when classes started at the end of August, college classes, she'd not only have these shoes (with her feet toughened up enough to wear them) but also a new outfit or two. She tapped her phone, scanning her bank account, and sighed. "Oh well, maybe just one new outfit. At least Mama can't say anything about my shoes. I bought them with my money."

Her aching feet enjoyed the cold floor. She watched the couple meander away from the ship. She stretched her back and lay on the bench, relaxing in the quiet, cold darkness and behind the stern glare the Goddess of Justice.

Luna sat up as a pang of awareness thumped into her stomach and rode her spine to her head. That pang had saved her more than once from Howard, the most obnoxious of the security guards, finding her resting when she should have been walking the floor *helping* visitors learn about *La Belle's* fatal voyage. But there was no one in the room.

The closing gong echoed, and Francine's voice returned, announcing the closing of the museum. As the last echo of Francine's voice entered her ears, she heard the faintest fall of shoe on the floor and a man's voice. "Expecting a trap?"

Luna covered her mouth with her hand. Her heart pounded in her chest, and she willed herself to silence despite the thunder of her heart in her ears. The man's voice didn't whisper, but it didn't carry as a voice should in the museum, silent except for the scuttling of shoes and murmurs filtering from the entrance.

A second masculine voice answered, "You're the one who always says to expect a trap but hope for honesty." This voice, while deep, wasn't as deep as the first. Both men spoke with peculiar accents: American but touched with something not European, not Asian, not Hispanic.

The first man replied, "None of us survive long without always thinking the worst of people, even old friends."

The second man laughed. "You never change, Max." The laugh should have echoed through the emptying museum, but it didn't. It drifted down, falling into Luna's ears like the water in a still pool.

Luna bit her bottom lip. Part of her job included guiding people to the exit at closing, and guests seldom gave her a hard time when she told them they had to leave. Neither man sounded in any hurry to leave. She looked at her shoes on the bench next to her.

Max said, "She's ugly."

Luna rolled her shoulders back and laughed to herself. Everyone said that about the Goddess of Justice.

"Not supposed to see her up close like this. At least that's what the guide says. Not sure I buy it," the other man said.

A heavy silence followed. Luna bent her head under its weight and focused her hearing on the landing.

"Cesar," said the deeper voice, Max's. So deep, so sure, yet fractured. "We have a problem."

"That's why we're meeting here," Cesar answered. "You're here to fix it, and you don't want anyone to know you're here."

Luna shivered at Cesar's response. His voice was filled with a loathing Luna had only heard one other time in her seventeen years. She rested her hand on her shoes, but she couldn't leave. She had to know what the problem was, even as the dread between the two men grew. A chill drifted down her back. Fear sank in her belly, but she didn't know why.

"What do you know?" Max asked.

"Nothing," Cesar answered. "An Eldest tells me she's sending you into town to take care of business. I don't ask questions."

"And that's why you'll live longer than most."

Luna held her breath even as her mouth formed the word Eldest.

When Max answered, Luna thought she imagined the words. "He kills children."

A groan—or perhaps a growl—gurgled from Cesar's mouth.

Max continued. "She sent me here because I've run into him before. I tracked him once and was close to seeing him, but he changes with the sun. It's nothing like I've ever seen."

"What do you need from me?" Cesar asked.

"For now, a reliable contact and anonymity," Max said.

Luna heard movement: leather brushing silk.

"Call Mike," Cesar said. "He's my go-to man, human. He'll get you whatever you need."

"Thanks," said Max.

"You won't stay unseen long. The others will feel your presence even if you try to hide from them," Cesar said.

Luna scrunched her eyebrows together. Curiosity overtook her caution, and she leaned forward, just enough to see the stairs. She could not see the two men.

"I'll take whatever time I can get. Let me know when we need to make this formal." Max sighed. "There's a chance it won't come to Austin."

But Max was certain it would. Luna heard that in the man's voice and felt the fear of it catch in her throat.

Cesar snorted. "If you believed that, you wouldn't be here. You're too good at what you do. Besides, Mary said—" Cesar's voice stopped.

Luna heard what could only be a sniff. Realizing she was standing, but not sure when she stood, she took a deep breath to calm herself, aware she had been holding her breath. That's when the pain shot up her leg from her right foot. She looked down to see red, sticky blood oozing out from between her toes. One of her blisters had burst.

"I've got this," Cesar said.

A chill, like the ceiling falling, descended on Luna. She wanted to move. Her heart beat so fast she couldn't catch her breath. Her brain screamed to run, but her feet remained where they were.

A hand rested on her shoulder. She turned, straining her neck to look up into the face of a man with the oddest of eyes. The man's face bent forward and his eyes, instead of peering into hers, looked like bright lights reflecting the spotlights from above.

"Hello, Luna," Max said. It could only be Max, with that melodious voice and rhythmic speech.

Luna reached for her name tag to cover it but found her hand wrapping around her neck instead.

Max smiled. His pale face relaxed and teeth, white and sharp, glistened in the light. "I wish you hadn't heard us talking," he said.

"Sorry," Luna's voice came out a coarse whisper, shaking in her breath.

"It's okay," he said. "But it's time to forget."

*****

"Luna! Wake up."

Luna sat up, her heart pounding like the voice in her ear, but the voice was Lisa's, her cousin. As she shook her head, another voice mingled with Lisa's, "Forget."

"Oh, Luna. You fell asleep on the bench again," Lisa said. "And look at your poor feet. Take this." Lisa handed Luna a white tea towel from her oversized handbag. "Use that to clean the blood off the floor. I've got another in my bag to clean your foot."

Luna leaned over and cringed at the sticky red blotches on the granite floor next to her shoes. It wasn't until she set her feet on the floor and pain shot through her toes that she remembered the blisters.

"I don't remember . . ." she muttered, reaching down to wipe away the sticky red pools.

Lisa dropped her large bag on the bench next to Luna and leaned her crutches on the bench as she lifted the clean left shoe.

Luna twisted to look at her cousin. "Thanks for waking me," she said. "I knew I was tired, but I didn't think—"

Lisa smiled as she twirled the shoe in her hand. "Oh, they are pretty. One day, I'll wear pretty shoes again." She set the shoe back on the floor next to its mate. "You're lucky I came in to look for you. Your mom would not be happy about you getting caught sleeping in the museum again. Mr. Jenkins said he'd fire you next time he caught you at it."

Luna handed the towel to Lisa, but Lisa pointed to another spot of blood, and Luna bent back over. "Why are you in here looking for me?"

"Wedding," Lisa answered, taking the dirty towel and handing Luna a clean one to wipe her feet. "I'm meeting with the bride and her mother here in another ten minutes. Aunt Jackie asked if I'd pick you up. Don't mind waiting, do you?"

Luna rolled her eyes. "If it keeps me out of the coffee shop, I'll wait here all night."

Lisa pursed her lips and shook her head.

A woman's voice called out, "Lisa?"

Lisa smiled. "Over here, Charlotte." Turning to Luna, she added, "That's my bride. You okay? You look a little . . . disheveled." Grabbing her crutches, Lisa pushed herself onto her good foot. "Have you met my cousin Luna? She's helping me out today."

Luna watched the figure of a too-thin woman walking toward them. The lights from the outer hall silhouetted her. Her figure reminded her of something or someone.

Luna shook her head. "What? I'm fine. Don't mind waiting. Do you have your other shoes in your bag?"

Lisa laughed. "I've got *your* sneakers in my bag. Aunt Jackie said you'd probably want them."

Luna grimaced. "What don't you have in that bag?"

Lisa used a crutch to point to her bag. "You can carry it for me."

Luna tied her shoes and watched as Lisa swung her bad leg forward and her crutches back in the mechanic yet somehow graceful pace she'd developed since breaking her leg last fall. The bones hadn't healed and might not, but neither cancer nor chemo had slowed Lisa.

Luna took Lisa's bag. "I got this," she said and followed her cousin.

*****

Luna lifted the bag and crossed the long strap over her chest. "How do you carry this around all day? It's killing my shoulders."

Lisa laughed, holding up one of her crutches. "You should carry it and use these things. Will you run upstairs and keep Charlotte and her mother from wondering around? In another half hour, they're going to kick us out of here."

Luna nodded, walking up the first flight of the staircase before Lisa finished asking. The bride, Charlotte, stood on the landing between the two flights, watching Luna. Her mother stood on the floor above.

"Mother," Charlotte said. "We have a problem."

Luna's foot stopped lifting her as the hairs on the back of her neck stood up. Her breath caught in her throat, but when she looked up, it was only Charlotte, an anxious bride.

Charlotte turned her face to look up at her mother. "If everyone is sitting on this side, they won't see me until I reach this point. My train is six feet long. They have to see it rising behind me for the full effect."

Luna exhaled, catching herself on the handrail as her lifting foot staggered. The weight of Lisa's bag tugged her forward, but she pulled herself back upright.

"Oh dear," said the mother. "Luna, are you all right?"

Luna nodded. "Just lost my footing for a sec. Thanks. I'm good."

Lisa hobbled to stand next to the mother. "Which is why we practice going down the stairs before the wedding."

Luna's lost footing forgotten, Lisa and Charlotte switched back to discussing the position of chairs and the importance of the Charlotte's train.

Luna froze, keeping a smile on her face and nodding whenever Lisa looked at her, but she didn't listen. The momentary fear lessened until she heard Lisa say, "Let's call Mike. He's my go-to man . . ." Lisa said something else, but Luna didn't hear.

Luna pulled a napkin from the pocket of Lisa's bag and wiped a bead of sweat forming on her forehead. She closed her eyes, but the words were not Lisa's.

"Darn," Lisa said. "He's already gone home, which means the museum folks will kick us out soon. Luna—"

Luna stared at Lisa, not hearing.

"Luna?" Lisa raised her voice.

Luna blinked. "Sorry. You need pictures. I'll get those." Luna pulled her phone out of her back pocket and started taking pictures of the staircase as Charlotte walked down.

*****

At Coffee Philosophy, Luna leaned over the pastry counter, tapping her finger at imaginary dots. Marcus cleaned the espresso machine, buffing the chrome until it reflected the dim overhead lights.

Luna sighed. "Why don't we close up early?"

Marcus scowled. "We have one more hour. I've been here all day, working to make money for the family. The least you could do is help for one more hour." He snatched the pile of towels he'd used to buff the espresso machine and stomped his feet through the door into the kitchen.

Luna rolled her eyes. "Whatever." She put her ear buds in and tapped to play a podcast, analyzing the day's news for Austin.

"Tropical Storm Barry became a category one hurricane today. Texas Gulf Coast residents are urged to stay alert. The National Weather Center expects Barry to turn toward the Louisiana coast. *There's a good chance it won't come to Austin.*"

Luna dropped the cup she'd picked up from a table.

The crash sent Marcus running in from the kitchen. "What?" he shouted.

A shudder of remembrance ran through Luna, and she looked up in time to see Marcus's lips press so tight she was sure he would break his jaw. His eyes widened.

Before either Luna or Marcus could say anything to each other, their mother, Jackie, opened the door from the office. "Everyone okay?"

"Yes, Mama," Luna said, bending down to pick up the broken pieces of the cup. "Sorry, Mama. The cup fell."

"Use the broom, Luna," Jackie said, smiling at Luna. "You don't want to cut yourself. Marcus, let's plan on inventory tomorrow."

Marcus closed his eyes and took in a deep breath. "Yes, Mama."

When Jackie returned to her office, closing the door behind her, Marcus grabbed the broom and dustpan from behind the coffee counter and threw them on the floor in front of Luna. "You never change," he whispered between clinched teeth.

Luna stretched her neck to look up at Marcus, saying nothing. The image of a man, no two men, and not images but shadows of men, stood above her, whispering. "He's killing children," one voice said. Her heart skipped a beat as a chilly hand rested on her shoulder, a hand that shouldn't have been so cold.

Marcus squared down to stare into Luna's eyes. He reached his hand out and touched her cheek. The warmth of his hand banished the chill, and she took in a deep breath. Marcus said, "I'm sorry."

Luna looked at the broken pieces of the cup scattered in front of her. She sniffed and wiped a tear away before it fell. "You're always sorry," she snapped.

Marcus picked up the broom and pushed the broken pieces into a mound. "I didn't mean to scare you."

The hurt was in his voice again. It was the same hurt she felt every time they fought. She picked up the dustpan and held it still as he wiped the broken bits into it. "I'm not sure I—" she didn't finish the sentence. It was too familiar. "I've got this," she said and stood.

"No," he said, taking the dustpan. "I'll take care of this. You have a customer." He nodded his head toward the back corner of the cafe, at the one table where no light shone.

Luna brushed her hands on her apron. The man leaned back in the chair. Long thin legs stretched out from under the table. As she approached, he leaned forward into the beam of the ceiling light. His pale face, long and lean like the rest of him, reflected the light back to her after first bouncing off sky-gray eyes that almost reflected the light from above.

The man smiled at her. "Good evening, Luna."

She stopped walking and narrowed her eyes.

The man smiled one of those small smiles, more than polite but not showing teeth. "I've been here some minutes and heard you talking. You're also wearing a name tag."

Luna tried to hold back the giggle, but it came out sounding like a snort. "Yeah," she said. "It's been one of those days. What can I get for you?"

"You decide," he said and leaned back in his chair. "Coffee and a pastry. You select your favorites."

Luna twisted to look behind her. Marcus stood with his arms crossed behind the coffee counter. She turned back to the man and leaned forward to whisper. "I don't like coffee, so I don't have a favorite, but Mamma says Marcus makes a good chocolate latte. Not sure what kind of pastries we have today. Aunt Jasmine brings them the first of the week. They won't be very fresh."

"Chocolate latte, it is," replied the man. "And pick the pastry you think would have the most carbs. Those are usually the best ones."

Luna nodded her head. "You got it."

Marcus went right to work making the chocolate latte as Luna used the tongs to squeeze the pastries on the display shelf.

"Luna!" snapped Marcus. "Don't pinch them all. You sure he didn't say what kind he wanted?"

Luna rolled her eyes. "Yes, I'm sure. And these are all old. We should have fresh pastries." She picked the least firm one and set it on a plate. "How do I warm it?"

"We'll get fresh ones in tomorrow. And you know how to warm up pastries. Stop playing stupid."

Luna grimaced. "I'm not stupid, you're just better at this." Luna stopped speaking and swung around to look at the man in the far corner. "Has he been in here before?"

Marcus placed the pastry in the oven and pressed the buttons. "Not as far as I know. Why?"

"Something familiar about him," Luna said.

The oven dinged, and she set the latte and pastry on a tray. Setting it on the table, she asked, "You've been in here before, haven't you?"

The man remained leaning back in the shadows. "Have I?"

"I should know who—"

She didn't finish her sentence. The man leaned forward. His eyes stared into hers. She'd never seen eyes so clear. His eyes looked into her and through her at the same time.

"Thank you, Luna," the man said. "I'm sure you don't know me."

Luna straightened her back, wondering why she slouched. "Call me if you need anything else."

At the coffee counter, Marcus leaned in close to whisper to her. "Well?"

"Well, what?" she asked, not whispering.

"Has he been here before?"

Luna shrugged her shoulders. "How would I know?"

She looked at the man as he tapped the screen of his phone. His face remained in darkness, and had she the eyesight of a hawk, she would have seen the text he sent.

"All is well. No memory."

Luna's Bad Day

"Where are my keys?" mumbled Eugene as she shifted the cushions and blankets on the living room couch. "Luna!" she shouted and looked up to see Luna leaning against the kitchen counter watching her. "Have you seen my keys?"

"Nope," Luna said. She straightened and turned to face the narrow staircase leading to the closed door of the computer room where Eugene did her tracing and hacking for CC. "You probably left them in your workroom. Want me to help you look up there?"

Eugene dashed past her, taking the old, narrow stairs two at a time. "You know the answer," she said and closed the door.

Luna sighed and stared at the closed door. She liked the painting Eugene had done of the wolf's face on the door, but she didn't like the four scars turning red to black across its face or the meadow green eyes, one with a scar that turned its green to a sickly white, staring at her when she stared up at the door. Or the way the teeth glistened as though they were ready to bite. It didn't help that the old servant's stair was dimly lit or that the old door rattled when anyone walked on the stairs. Eugene said the painting was a warning to other wolves. Luna thought it was meant for her; nevertheless, she liked the painting.

Shrugging, she turned and poured coffee into the large red mug covered with daisies her brother had given her for Christmas. Holding the mug to her nose, she breathed in the coffee beans with their hints of vanilla, chocolate, and earth. Her mouth watered. She giggled. Last year, she didn't like coffee. This year, since she'd stopped working in the family coffee shop every day, she loved a good cup of coffee sweetened with honey and just the right amount of cream.

Opening the refrigerator in the tiny kitchen, she laughed, hearing Eugene stomp around her little room. Something fell on the floor and she yelled, "Damn it all to hell! Where are my keys?"

Luna stopped laughing as the stench of rancid cream slapped her in the face, running into her nose, down her throat, and into her gut. She slammed the door closed as the stench churned her stomach, shooting acid into her throat.

"Luna," moaned Eugene, opening the door. "What did you kill?"

"I bought cream yesterday. Package must have been mislabeled," Luna answered between gags.

"Don't leave it in the fridge. Get it outside. I still can't find my keys," Eugene grumbled, jumping down the stairs and returning to her search in the living room.

Luna steeled her resolve. She stood still, studying the door to the refrigerator, imagining where the offensive cream sat on the top shelf. At last, she took a deep breath, opened the door, grabbed the thin carton, and ran out the back door. Outside, she could breathe with only hints of rancid cream drifting into her nose.

"What now?" she asked no one. She stepped, almost tripping, down the steps and into the fenced area surrounding the garbage cans for the houses on this block. All the houses in the area were also businesses, and since the lockdown began, few cars sat in the small parking area. It was the first time in weeks Luna was glad for the lockdown. Normally, despite the signs, someone always managed to park between the door and the trash cans, blocking easy access. Today, she had a smooth run to them.

The trash cans, however, sat so stuffed their lids would not close. She lifted the lid to the least-full can and set the container on top, letting the lid plop down, then jumped backwards as rancid cream squished out of the container, barely missing her. The smell billowed over the wooden fence. She grimaced and hoped it would rain. Soon.

Satisfied with her diligent effort to keep the kitchen clean, she went back into the house. Her cup sat on the counter. "Eugene, want a cup of coffee? I can't drink it without cream."

"Thanks," Eugene said, grabbing the cup as she walked into the tiny kitchen. "You should learn to drink it black, like me. I'm going to check my room. Can't believe I can't find my keys."

Luna sighed as the aroma from the coffee pot tempted her. Face downcast, she followed Eugene through the swinging door between the kitchen and the reception room. Luna liked her large old-fashioned desk sitting between CC's office and Mike's. She'd thought CC and Mike had offered her the job in order to monitor her, but when CC showed her the desk and computer, how to access files and use the phone, and let her talk to clients, she realized she was needed. She enjoyed the work and liked to speculate what her days would be like when Mike returned from his vacation with Stanley. They'd surprised no one when they announced they'd married over the Christmas break. Then they'd taken a trip to New Zealand, but no one foresaw the pandemic keeping them in New Zealand.

Eugene's long legs took the stairs in the once-grand staircase leading to the second floor two at a time. Eugene ran everywhere, never walked, unless she was sleeping. Only then was she still. Luna shook her head, laughing at Eugene but admiring her wolf-like grace and dexterity.

"Ow!" shouted Eugene.

Luna looked up at the landing. "You okay?"

"Just stubbed my toe on a chair leg," Eugene said, sliding the chair next to the table of flowers on the landing into place.

Luna's computer alarm dinged. Before she reached her computer, Eugene leaned over the railing. "Luna, you set out the milk and cookies last night, didn't you?"

Luna's eyes widened. She opened her mouth, thinking of the best answer, then nodded. "Of course. It's time for my call with Mike."

She sat down and clicked the link in the pink box on her calendar. The screen flashed black, then blue, before the calendar returned and Mike's face smiled at her.

"Hi Luna. How's it going?"

*****

After ten minutes of instructions, Luna rolled her eyes and sighed with boredom. "I got it, Mike. Don't worry. The courthouse opened a window for essential business. Checked it out on my way home yesterday. I'll be there first thing in the morning and get the papers filed."

"And not leave until you see the stamp on them, right? Luna, if a judge doesn't see the official stamp, a lot of money will disappear. You don't want me explaining to Cesar why the papers weren't filed on time, do you?" asked Mike.

"Hey, Luna," shouted Phineas, Eugene's twin brother, as he jogged in from the back of the house into the reception room. "What are you still doing here?" He stopped and leaned over Luna's shoulder. "Hey, Mike. Still liking New Zealand?"

Luna punched Phineas's chest. "Do you mind? You're covered with germs."

Phineas rolled his eyes. "You can't get sick. You know—"

"CC can." Luna stood, pulling a can of Lysol from her desk drawer. She aimed it at him, and he straightened as she sprayed him.

"In full control of the office, I see," said Mike. "Don't take it so hard, Phin. Stanley's just as bad. I even taste Lysol in my food."

Phineas rolled his eyes. "Tell me about it. Sorry, but I gotta run," Phineas said. "We'll talk later."

Phineas ran up the stairs and tripped halfway up. "Damn it! Luna, why didn't you tell me the carpet was coming up on the stairs."

Luna sighed. "How am I supposed to know that? I don't live here, and you remind me daily I'm not allowed upstairs."

Static lines filled Luna's monitor. She banged the edge with her palm until the static cleared. "He's been nothing but cranky since he started taking on extra shifts at the clinic," she said as Mike's face returned to the screen. "Sorry you're not seeing much of New Zealand."

Mike shrugged. "Got to see Hobbiton before lockdown. Now, about those papers. You don't do anything first thing in the morning. Maybe I should talk to Eugene about getting them turned in. The entire schedule is out of whack if they're not. Now, show me again their order in the packet." Mike tapped his screen and added. "And why *are* you in the office? Isn't it after quitting time there?"

"Laptop quit on me this morning," Luna said. "Eugene said she'd look at when she gets time. I wouldn't have to stay, but my history prof is doing a lecture tonight. If I don't sit in live, I have to watch the replay, and I never get around to watching the replays. I hate online classes."

Luna sighed and picked up the packet of legal documents. Before she could speak, Eugene yelled from the back of the house. "Luna! You didn't take out Bean. Now there's pee on the kitchen floor. You know Chihuahuas have little bladders."

Luna straightened in her chair and twisted toward the swinging door. "He's your dog—"

CC opened the door of her private office, interrupting her. "Eugene! Luna," she shouted. "What have I said about yelling in the house during business hours?"

Luna pointed to the time on top of her monitor. "It's after hours."

"Hi, CC," called out Mike, overtaking her voice.

CC moved to stand behind Luna. She smiled and waved. "Hi Mike. How's lockdown in New Zealand?"

"The same as it would be there, only the New Zealanders take it seriously."

"I wish more around here did. I'm more than a little stir crazy. Hang on a sec." CC lifted her hand to stop Mike from saying anything. She turned to face Luna. "Where are those papers I told you to put on my desk?"

"On your desk," Luna said. "Put them there when I got in."

"They're not there now. Print them out again. Sorry, Mike," she said. "Love to talk, but I need to get dressed. Give Stanley my love."

"She's got a date with Cesar," Luna said, winking at Mike.

"It's not a date," yelled CC from the stairs. "It's business."

Luna nodded to Mike. "Newcomers to Austin. She and Cesar are coordinating their histories. Getting a lot in these days."

"Luna," said Mike, pinching his lips so hard the scar on the side of his face turned white. "There are certain topics we don't mention on calls?"

"Oh please," Luna said with a huff. "With Eugene's set-up, who's getting in to listen?"

"It doesn't matter—" Mike started.

"Where are my keys?" shouted Eugene from the back room.

Phineas jumped over the last three stairs, landing with his usual wolffish grace. "Any coffee, Luna?" he asked as he headed for the swinging door to the back.

"Luna," shouted Eugene, pushing the swinging door open. Her mug of coffee preceded her head and hit Phineas's chest, spilling its contents down his front.

"Hot!" Phineas squeezed out from between lips pressed tight.

"Oh, bro," Eugene said. "So sorry. I was bringing you coffee. I meant for you to drink it, but if you'd rather wear it . . ." Eugene smirked and bit her lower lip to not laugh.

Luna pulled a roll of paper towels out from under her desk and jumped up to hand them to Phineas.

"Thank you," he said, his jaw still clamped shut. "This was my last clean set of scrubs."

"Oh," said Eugene, smiling. "I did a load of laundry earlier. Let me see if I can put them in the dryer, but then I need to eat and get back to work."

"Thought you had time in the studio today?" asked Phineas, patting his shirt dry with paper towels.

"Later," yelled Eugene, pushing through the door again and heading to the kitchen. Even out of the room, she continued to talk loudly so everyone would hear her. "I don't mind getting the late hours. That's the best part of the whole social distancing thing. Only a couple of us can be in the studio at one time. I get it practically all to myself when I take the late hours."

"Social distancing suc—is boring," said Luna. "My first year in college, and I don't get to go to a real class or go to any parties." She jumped as a high-pitched squeal of feedback poured out of the speakers on her computer.

Phineas, still standing near her desk, and Eugene, from the kitchen, both yelled, "Ow!"

Luna put her hands over her ears. "Mike?" she yelled, pressing keys on her keyboard until the squeal disappeared.

"Luna?" Mike's voice asked. The picture disappeared.

"On no!" Eugene shouted from the back of the house. "The washer crapped out. There's water everywhere. Phin! Come help me clean this up before CC sees it."

Mike and Phineas asked, almost at the same time, "Luna, did you forget to leave the milk and cookies out?"

Luna closed her eyes as a lump of coal landed in her gut. "Guys," she whined.

"Eugene," Phineas called. "I'm coming. Luna forgot to leave out the milk and cookies last night."

Eugene's head popped into the reception room before Phineas could leave. "You forgot to leave out the milk and cookies," she said. "Again? If I don't find my keys in the next ten minutes, you're paying me for my lost tips."

"Luna," Mike said. "It's not your day, is it?"

*****

Luna crossed her arms. "What's the big deal about leaving a saucer of milk and a few cookies out every night?"

"It's one of your duties as Administrative Assistant," Mike said.

"But why?"

"Hey!" shouted CC from upstairs. "Who turned on the washer? I'm taking a shower."

"Sorry, CC," Luna said, jumping out of her chair and pushing the swinging door open. "Eugene, turn off the washer. CC's showering."

"Oops! Sorry, CC," Eugene yelled. "At least it's working, but now the dryer won't turn on."

Phineas pushed Luna out of the way and headed for the stairs. "I'm going up to put on a clean shirt," he grumbled, then tripped on the stair with the loose carpet and banged the same shin he'd bruised earlier. "Satisfied, Luna? Now I'll be late back to the clinic."

"Want a salad, Phin?" Eugene yelled from the back.

"Yeah," said Phineas, ignoring Luna's widening eyes.

"Mike," she said, but the front door opened. She sat up and smiled. "Hi, Ramon." On the screen, Mike winked at her, and she blushed. "Here to pick up CC? She's running a bit late."

Ramon, his nose and mouth covered by a blue paper mask, shrugged and sprawled in one of the guest chairs. He grabbed a magazine off the side table and opened it in front of his face.

Luna sighed and stared at the magazine cover. "You know, you don't need to wear a mask here."

Without lowering the magazine, Ramon replied, "Cesar said to be the model conscientious citizen. So, I am."

"Luna," came Mike's voice. "We were talking."

Luna shook her head. "Oh, yeah. Sorry. Set out the milk and cookies every night, no matter what. Got it. Your packet's ready. I'll take it over in the morning and won't leave until I see each page stamped *received*. I should go. Lecture starts soon."

"Luna." Mike huffed, took in a deep breath, and shrugged. "It's up to you to make things right. Better do it soon."

"Bye," Luna said without looking at Mike and clicked the end call button.

"Urgh!" Eugene's voice echoed. "Every bag of salad has gone bad. Luna!" Eugene opened the door. "This is why we set out milk and cookies every night. What am I going to do now? I've been delivering fattening, greasy food all day. I'm starving."

"Come with me," said Phineas. He stopped halfway down the stairs and jumped over the rail, landing on his feet as always, but he kept his eyes fixed on Ramon. "Let's pick up something from the cafe. We can walk."

Ramon lowered the magazine and stared at Phineas with narrowing eyes. Eugene pushed the swinging door open as she pulled her backpack onto her back.

"Hi, Ramon." The strap of her backpack broke, sending the open backpack and its contents onto the ground. A bottle of ink flew toward Ramon. He raised his hand, catching it, even as a second bottle fell at Luna's feet. It shattered, spraying glass and black ink onto her new white sneakers.

"Urgh!!!" shouted Eugene. "I've had enough. It's your fault," she said, turning to Luna. Her eyes narrowed and her lips twitched. "You clean up your mess. Text me when it's done."

"Aren't you going to fix my laptop?" asked Luna.

Eugene tugged Phineas's arm, leading him to the front door. "No point. Until you fix your mess, it'll just break again."

"Luna," said CC from the head of the stairs. "Have you reprinted those documents for me? Hi, Ramon. I'll be there in a jiff."

"Take your time, Ms. Carson," Ramon muttered and lifted the magazine back in front of his face.

Luna clicked her mouse and opened the file with CC's documents. She hit the print button. The printer on the side of her desk clanked once, twice, and spat out page after page with nothing but a thick black line down the center.

"No!" Luna squealed. "No! Don't quit on me now."

"Should have left the milk and cookies out last night," Ramon said from behind the magazine.

*****

"What's the big deal about leaving out a bowl of milk and a few cookies?" cried Luna. Her bottom lip shook as she tried again to stop the printer.

Ramon dropped the magazine onto the side table. "You're either the densest chick I know or just stupid."

"I'm not stupid!" Luna answered, slapping the desk with her hand. "Mike said it was for a goblin, but there's no such thing as goblins."

Ramon shook his head. "And there's no such thing as werewolves, but you know two of them, and they live upstairs."

Luna puckered her lips and tilted her head. "Yeah. There is that."

"And there's no such thing as vampires."

"Yeah," replied Luna, tilting her head in the other direction. She squinted and stared at Ramon. "You're one, aren't you?"

Ramon shook his head again. "You are dense."

"I am not!" Luna said, standing and hitting an open drawer with her shin. "Ow!"

Ramon sighed. "I don't get paid enough for this," he muttered.

"What?" Luna said, bending over to rub her shin. The paper drawer on the printer fell out of the printer and hit her in the head. "Oh, give me a break! I'm new to all of this." She sat down, rubbing her forehead, and took a deep breath as her eyes watered. "That's going to leave a bruise."

Ramon stood and walked to her desk. He pulled a tissue from the box on her desk and handed it to her.

Luna grabbed the tissue and blew her nose. "I'm not crying. It's the hit on the head."

He sat on the edge of her desk and pulled his mask off. "I suppose I'll get out of here faster if you make nice with the goblin. When I was told I was going to be Cesar's new driver, I didn't know I'd have to be a babysitter too." He folded his arms across his chest. "Look, it's like this. There's a goblin living somewhere in this house. Probably in the attic. They like attics." He lifted his palm to Luna as her mouth opened. "Don't ask me why. I don't know. From what I'm seeing here, I'm guessing he's one of those who does nice things for the inhabitants."

"Nice," interrupted Luna. "What's he doing nice today?"

"Let me finish," Ramon said, standing and putting his hands in his pants pockets. "They fix things, make a good guard when you're away, and they take nothing that's not offered to them."

Luna sniffled and continued to stare at him.

He rolled his eyes. "Dense. They take nothing at all, not even food. If you don't leave out something for them to eat, they get cranky."

"Oh," said Luna. She nodded her head and smiled. "I just need to feed him."

"Something like that."

Luna stood and pushed open the door to the kitchen.

"By now," said Roman, stopping her, "he's turned not just the salad and the milk but anything else you might offer him bad."

Luna's face dropped. Her watch binged an alarm. "Then what am I going to do? My lecture starts in five minutes, and CC needs those documents for Cesar. She's going to kill me, and I'll totally forget to watch the replay of the lecture. I'll get a zero, and then—"

Roman raised his hands in surrender as his face relaxed and a smile lifted the corners of his mouth. It was the first time Luna had ever seen a smile on his face. His silver eyes twinkled, and this time, it wasn't the lamps in the room reflecting in his large clear-brown eyes. "I got you covered," he said and pulled a candy bar from his inner jacket pocket. "Consider this a peace offering."

Luna took the candy bar. "Peace offering? I didn't know we were fighting."

"We're not." He nodded. "But I'm stuck here until your boss gets what she needs so I can drive her to Cesar's for dinner. And unless you make nice with your goblin, none of us are going anywhere."

"Got it," said Luna, her mouth widening, but just as suddenly as she grinned, she frowned. "How do I give it to the goblin? I've been setting the milk and cookies out when I leave. I've never seen him."

"Call him. They don't like those outside the house seeing them, so I'll step outside." He walked out the front door. Before closing the door, he pulled his mask back up and added, "Be careful. Most goblins are tricksters. Negotiate well."

Luna stared at the closing door. "You'd better not be pulling a prank on me," she muttered to herself. Taking a deep breath, she called out, "Hey, Goblin."

*****

"I knew it," she muttered after a few moments passed with no response. "Nothing."

"Well?" came a coarse voice, deep and small at the same time. "What do you want?"

Luna's face dropped. Sitting on the bottom stair was a moss-colored goblin with dark-green eyes, thinning shaggy brown hair hanging down below his neck and combed over the top of his head, pointed ears sticking up over the top of his head, and lobes pulled low with multiple gold rings hitting his shoulders. He wore a loud blue suit with a gold and red striped vest over a green shirt and tie. Dark green boots with pointed toes tapped the floor with impatience.

"You're a goblin," Luna said, falling backwards in her chair. Her mouth remained open, eyes fixed on the goblin.

"Hobgoblin," corrected the goblin. He scratched a thin brown beard on his chin. "And you're a human. Now that we've established species, what the hell do you want?"

"Oh," Luna closed her mouth and looked down at her hand holding the candy bar. "I'm sorry about not leaving milk and cookies out for you last night."

The goblin sniffed. "Of course you are. Everyone's sorry when it's too late." He stood and walked toward her, stopping three feet in front of her.

Luna looked down to stare at his eyes as he pointed his finger at her. "Look, I didn't ask for this gig. I was sent here to protect the house. And what thanks do I get? Do I look like a freaking ten-year-old? Ha! You're a waste of my talents. I should leave before you drown me with more milk and cheap cookies."

Luna continued to stare into the goblin's eyes. They were like black crystals full of sharp edges, glittering as he spoke. His crooked mouth smirked under a long pointed nose. Luna followed the edges of his thick sideburns to see if his mouth was truly crooked or if he was just a bad shaver.

"Who sent you here?" she asked.

"The boss. Who else? Now what do you want? I'm getting out of here, but you called me."

Luna grinned. "So, you'll need the boss to approve you leaving here?" Her smile widened as the goblin's nose twitched.

"Not a problem," he said. He held up his right hand and crossed all five fingers at once. "Me and the boss, we're like this. I can go any time I want. Boss'll get some other sucker to keep an eye on things."

"Oh," said Luna, nodding her head. "I understand. It was very rude of me to not set out the milk and cookies. I'm very sorry." Her fingers tapped the candy bar in her hands. "Oh my gosh! Where are my manners? What's your name?"

The goblin put his hands on his hips. "Why do you want to know?"

"Well . . ." She looked over his head to the stairs. CC stood on the top stair leaning on the banister, watching. "You see, I was taught it was rude to make an apology and not even know the name of the person you're apologizing to."

The goblin scratched his chin again. "Whatever," he said. "Apologies don't pay the rent. I'm out of here."

Luna nodded, lifting the candy bar to her face and holding it in both hands, twirling it, so the name of it flashed down to the goblin. "I understand. I even got you this hoping you'd forgive me for being so rude."

"Butterfinger, eh?" The goblin reached a hand up to take the candy bar but stopped as Luna turned from him and put the candy bar in her desk drawer.

"It was nice to meet you," Luna said, not looking at him. "Best of luck on your next assignment."

"Well," the goblin said. "I should take into consideration your youth and inexperience." The goblin moved to stand next to Luna.

Luna bit her lip to resist the urge to turn her head and look into his strange face.

The goblin continued, "If I've been a bit harsh, well, I suppose I could be forgiven for assuming the worst of you, but I see now you're a good person—for a human, that is."

"I try to be," Luna said, nodding and shuffling the documents on her desk from one side to the other. "I knew going to college would open up new worlds to me, but I had no idea what a goblin—oh, sorry. I had no idea what a hobgoblin was or that one lived in the house where I work. I have so much to learn." Luna stopped shuffling papers and looked at the front door. "The vamps will teach me all I need to know. And Eugene is good at explaining things when she's not—"

The goblin erupted. "Vamps! And Werewolves! They don't know shit about keeping the worlds flowing in the right direction."

Luna opened the desk drawer in front of the goblin's face and pulled out a folder. "Excuse me, but it's not nice to swear."

The goblin grunted and pinched his face as though he would explode. He stared at Luna, who wasn't paying attention to him. "Cobalt's the name," he said, holding out his hand. "Pleased to make your acquaintance, Luna."

Luna shook hands with Cobalt. "So," she said. "I suppose things will stop going wrong now that we're friends."

Cobalt's eyes shifted from Luna's face to her desk drawer. He bit his lip and shook his head. "Seeing as we're friends, and you meant no disrespect. I certainly didn't."

"Everything will work now, and no one else will get bruised," Luna added.

Cobalt still stared at the drawer, his head bobbing up and down. "Yeah, yeah, but you know, milk and cookies get boring after a while."

Luna opened the drawer, taking out the candy bar. "I could do something about that, seeing as we're going to be friendly and you're going to teach me about how the worlds flow." She offered him the candy bar. "We're good?"

Cobalt snatched the candy bar from Luna's hand. "Deal," he said and vanished.

Luna clicked her mouse, and her class opened. The professor was checking roll and said, "Oh, hello Luna. Nice to see you again." As his face disappeared and his slide show started, Luna walked into CC's office and found the papers she'd prepared for CC on a side table. She put them in a folder and went back to her desk.

CC walked down the stairs. Luna held up the folder for her. "Here you go. Just the way you wanted them."

CC smiled and her eyes widened. "Thanks, Luna."

Luna sat down, but before she could pick up a pen and take any notes, CC bent over and hugged her.

"I'm not used to him being here either," she whispered into Luna's ear. "Thanks for fixing things."

Luna's jaw fell open. "You—"

"Didn't ask him here, but I have a pretty good idea who did. Lock up when you leave." CC put the folder into her backpack, then opened the front door. "I'm ready, Ramon."

Luna jumped out of her chair, pulling a mask from the stack next to the door. "Don't forget this."

Ramon stood on the walkway leading to the street. He nodded but said nothing.

Eugene walked in, carrying a white box. "Here you go."

Phineas, following, smiled. "Didn't want you to go hungry."

Back at her desk, Luna opened the box to find her favorite pimento and cheese sandwich and a cup of piping hot tomato soup. She leaned back in her chair, listening to her history professor and watching slides about the battle of San Jacinto. Her foot hit something cold and hard. She reached down and pulled up a ring of keys with a Vegas sign attached to it.

"Eugene," she yelled. "Found your keys."

She pulled a paper plate out from a bottom drawer and placed half her sandwich on it. "Tomorrow, we should have tacos. Chili after that," she muttered and leaned back in her chair. She put her hands behind her head and her feet on the desk. "Altogether," she said. "Not a bad day."

Memories of a Kiss

Danita stepped onto the hot evening sidewalk. As the car drove away, she removed an ear loop of her mask, letting it hang free as she breathed in the tangy scent of rain and a summer storm. She tapped her phone. The forecast still said clear skies and only an eighteen percent chance of rain. She shook her head and examined the street. The houses were old, perhaps over a hundred years old. The front lawns were small, well-manicured patches with masses of summer roses, gardenias, boxwoods, and like the house in front of her, crepe myrtles. Signs announcing legal, accounting, and other professional services stood inside neat little fences, while the blue light of televisions glowing through curtains indicated the houses were also homes. Across the street, a dog park stretched the full block, separating this block from student housing scattered on the opposite side of the park. She could have walked from her office on campus, but it was the end of a long day, and the University would reimburse her for the ride.

Reaching under the hem of her jacket, she tugged her blouse to pull it down. She then twisted, checking the pleat of her skirt and shifting it until the flap was centered between her knees before stepping onto the short walkway between two rows of crepe myrtles pushing out their first blooms of summer. A gust of wind blew pink petals into her thick, dark hair as her stiletto heels tapped on the concrete walkway. Two brass plaques hung on the side wall of the vestibule. On one sign: *Mike Young, Attorney*; the other: *Carson Security Consultants*. She raised her eyebrows. "Does he rent a room here?"

As she reached for the shining brass door handle, it turned blue as the dark screen above it glowed to life, revealing a touchpad and camera. "Oh," she breathed in. "Very sleek." Then she saw the small plastic sign reading "Please Enter" taped to the solid, dark oak door. Danita pulled her mask into place, checking the tension in the straps over her ears, and that the nose clip was well-fitted over the bridge of her nose, and pushed the door open.

In front of her, a staircase led to the second floor. She stepped inside. To the right of the stairs, a large antique wooden desk with three computer monitors sat empty. A swinging door behind it opened. A young woman in blue-jean cut-offs and a Longhorn T-shirt walked into the room, carrying a brown Chihuahua. The young woman looked up with a smile and wide eyes. "Hi," she said.

Danita waited as the woman sat and placed the small dog in the center of the desk. The room was obviously a reception room—neat, well dusted, a bit old-fashioned with heavy blue drapes enclosing the large garden window Danita noticed when she arrived, but the young woman showed no sign of receiving her.

Danita looked again at the address on her phone and cleared her throat. "Excuse me, but I'm looking for Eugene Plumb."

"Oh, gosh. Sorry," the young woman said, looking up. "She's out of town. Can I help you?"

Danita shook her head. "That's not possible. He was at work this afternoon and is due back at work tomorrow."

"Oh," the woman said. She grinned and almost laughed. "You want Phineas. No one ever comes to see him. My bad."

Danita opened her mouth to object when the young woman laughed. "Confusing, I know. Twins with the same first name. Silly, isn't it? His middle name is Phineas, and that's what we call him around here."

At that moment, a tall man wearing only faded jeans, tight with the top button resting dead center on his groin, leaped from the stairs over the railing to land in front of her.

"Phin!" said the woman at the desk. "Do you always have to do that?" The small dog broke into a series of loud yaps.

The man looked down at Danita with the darkest, deepest brown eyes she'd ever seen. They glowed in the room's light. "Sorry," he said. His voice flowed from deep inside his throat. "I heard my name, but I was just getting out of the shower and didn't realize I had company."

Danita tried not to stare, but his wide chest and slim waist glistened with dampness across sun-tanned skin molded tight over muscles that rippled like a wave with each breath he took. His biceps rolled like the tide as he pulled a white T-shirt over his head and tucked it under his waistband.

He bent over the reception desk. "Let me have Bean, Luna. You know CC doesn't want him in the reception area." He turned back to Danita. "Sorry," he said. His eyes danced as he smiled, revealing long, lovely white teeth.

"No problem, —Mr. Plumb," she said before coughing and opening her briefcase. "You haven't signed the release papers for Dr. Antoin." She stumbled over her words, but looking at the papers, she took in a deep breath and returned to business. "For the article about you to appear in our newsletter. We want very much to run the article. You're a role model for the new PA program. Oh!" She stopped and pulled a business card out of her pocket. "I'm Danita Soliz, Secretary to the Director of Communications for the University Medical System."

Luna snickered. "Right, role model."

Danita darted her eyes to Luna's and cleared her throat. "Perhaps I could have something to drink."

Luna's eyes widened as she stood, and her welcoming grin turned up at one corner as one of her eyebrows lifted. "Oh, sure," she said. "Tea or coffee? Water?"

"A cup of tea would be very nice," Danita said, nodding. "Thank you."

Phineas winked at Danita as Luna walked past him. "Have a seat, Ms. Soliz," he said, pointing Danita to a chair in front of the blue-draped garden window.

"Danita. Please call me Danita," she said, resisting the urge to wink back at him.

Phineas took the papers from Danita's hand and set them on the small table between them as he settled with the little dog on his lap. "I'm sorry you felt you had to come here, but I spoke to someone in Dr. Antoin's office this afternoon. I don't want an article about me in the newsletter."

Danita removed her mask and smiled at Phineas. "So modest," she said. "It's very attractive, which adds to Dr. Antoin's choice of you as the model—for the new program. He's very passionate about the project. So am I."

Phineas nodded. "I'm sure. Updating the Physician's Assistants program opens it up to more people, but I'm not the model for you. Now, my friend Rob? He puts in as many hours as I do, and he's a UT grad. He's perfect for your article."

"Rob?" Danita asked. A chill ran down her back, and she sat up. She shivered but shook her head to chase it away. "His last name? The physicians I spoke with all recommended you, but I recall the name Rob now, or perhaps Robert?"

"Glad to know they like me. Yes, it's Robert." He pulled his phone out of his back pocket. "Let me send you his info."

Danita's heart skipped a beat. "Here's my e-card. It has my cell on it. I'm very easy to get hold of."

Thunder erupted around them, shaking the windows. Rain poured onto the roof, and the wind rattled the windows. Danita turned to the covered window behind her. "Oh!" she squealed. "Weathermen! They never get it right."

Phineas stood and pulled the curtains apart enough to look outside. The little dog snuggled close to his chest and licked his chin. "Then it's a good thing Luna brought out the tea tray. Enjoy your cup. I'm sure it will pass soon. I'm sorry, Danita, but I really don't want that article to be about me."

Another rumble of thunder rattled her eardrums, and the lights went out.

"No!" shouted Luna. "I've got an—exam tonight."

"Just wait," said Phineas. "The generator will kick in soon."

"Oh," murmured Luna. "Will you stay and make sure we have internet?"

"You know I will."

The lamp on the reception desk and the lamp next to Danita turned on.

"You see," said Phineas. "Generator's already kicking in. I'll head up and check the computers. You two sit here and relax."

Phineas pushed the swinging door, but before walking through, he turned back to Luna. "You better lock up, Luna. It's late, and no one we want to see will come in this storm."

Luna grumbled but set the tray on the little table as Danita picked up the paperwork.

"Thank you," Danita said, looking at the neatness of the tray with its pot and matching cups and a plate of large chocolate chip cookies. She smiled up at Luna, who stared at the tray with her head cocked to the side. "I hope you will be able to *take your exam*. It must be a mean professor who makes you take an exam on a Friday night."

Luna snickered. "Eugene's got this super system here. We never lose net. That's one reason I take my exams here. CC doesn't mind as long as I do it after hours. But really, this place is always open, so it's not like I can block off time just for me." Luna drooped her head to her shoulder and pointed to Danita's neck. "That's pretty."

"Oh." Heat washed over Danita's face as her fingers touched the gold button on its black silk ribbon tied at her neck. "A little good luck charm I picked up somewhere."

Luna put a finger to her lips. "Looks familiar, but I can't place it. Too dark to see it well."

Thunder cracked again, smashing into the house. Danita startled in her seat. "A very big storm. It's the ones that are so sudden that frighten me."

Luna pointed to the swinging door. "We're safe and snug here. Nothing bad happens in this house. Stay until it passes. I like your suit."

Danita poured water from the pitcher into a cup without looking at Luna. "Thank you. Your boss doesn't mind?" She stopped and looked up. "What kind of exam do you take on a Friday night?"

Even in the darkened room, Danita could see Luna's cheeks darken.

"Well," Luna began. "I suppose I could have taken it earlier."

"You didn't heat the water," Danita said, lifting her cup.

"Dang, blast it!" Luna said, puckering her mouth and pounding her fist into the table. "Knew I forgot something. I'm so sorry. CC picked out this set just for clients, and I had it all set up. I even picked up cookies on my way here tonight. I guess with my mov—exam and the power out, my mind just isn't working." Luna sighed as her face and shoulders drooped.

Danita stood, picking up the tray, and laughed. She let the laugh linger, easing the tension in the air. As Luna's cheeks returned to normal, she said, "You're new to professional work. You're the secretary?"

Luna's face widened with a smile. "Administrative Assistant. I don't normally do tea, coffee, that sort of thing. Not that I mind. Learned how to do it right at the family coffee shop. Mama always insisted everything be done right, but—"

Danita's laughter stopped Luna's speech. "I like you, Luna. You remind me of me when I was younger." She stepped toward Luna. "I'm a secretary. Secretary to the Director of Communications for the entire University Medical System. I've worked very hard. I make tea and coffee all the time, not because Dr. Antoin asks or expects me to, but because my services help very busy people doing very important work. Oh, the stories I could tell you over the past year, like when poor Dr. Antoin caught COVID. But first, let's make tea. We'll use the storm as an excuse for me to be here a little longer. These cookies are very good. You must tell where you got them."

Thunder shook the building again. The two lamps blinked off as the front door swung open, letting in an icy rush of wind. Danita, startled as icy rain blasted her face, screamed. The tray crashed to the floor, the lid of the teapot falling off, spilling water across the floor as the cups shattered into pieces.

In the doorway stood a tall, thin man dressed in black. Long hair dripped down his face and neck. "Where's Phineas?"

Luna put her hands on her hips. "Max? Will you stop making an entrance? Look at what you broke this time."

*****

The two lamps flashed to life again as the swinging door opened and Phineas stepped into the reception room. A deep, growling voice echoed in the silent room. "What's wrong?"

The little dog in the back room yapped louder and louder as it rushed into the room between Phineas's feet. A large white dog poked its head around Phineas's legs. Danita stared at the wet white teeth gleaming from a white muzzle as pink eyes reflected the desk lamp, turning them blood red.

Luna pointed to the back room. "You two," she said, pointing to the two dogs. "Stay back there."

Max stepped into the house, closing the door. He glanced once at Danita and nodded to Luna before motioning to Phineas, who led him to a door on the far side of the room. The large white dog followed them.

As the door closed, the icy chill on Danita's spine slid off her back. She breathed in the damp, wet summer storm and put her hand on Luna's shoulder. "Perhaps we should give the two gentlemen a little space."

Luna nodded but squinted, staring at the door the two men went through. "That's CC's office." She pulled a trash can out from under her desk. "I'll clean this up. Please, go on into the living room. Fluffy, the big dog, isn't there to bother you."

Danita reached out and took Luna's hand in hers. "I'll help. First, show me to the kitchen? I'll make us tea, and then we'll come out and clean this up. That's a good plan. Don't you think?"

Luna looked into Danita's face. "Yes," she said, nodding her head. "Watch your step." Before Luna opened the swinging door, she called out, "Bean, come," and the little dog followed them.

Danita followed Luna into a wide living room with a sofa and chairs to her right in front of a massive television screen. A cluttered island separated the living room and a galley kitchen that disappeared behind the closet under the stairs she had seen when she walked into the house. An empty kettle sat on the apartment-sized stove top. Danita filled it with water as she explained the proper temperature needed to make a good cup of tea.

"Dr. Antoin, that's my boss. He likes black tea, strong, with plenty of cream and sugar. You would never guess it by looking at him. Much too thin for a man. Me, I like a thin man, but he needs curves and ripples in all the right places—rather like our friend who jumps over stair railings."

Danita winked and smiled as Luna giggled. She continued, "It must be nice to have a generator when storms like this—"

Phineas's shout interrupted her. "When did this happen?"

Danita froze with one hand on the kettle handle and another on the gas dial to turn on the flame.

"Something's happened," Luna said. Like Danita, she stared toward CC's office as though they could see through the walls.

"Yes," said Danita. "Never stand around waiting for a pot to boil. Let's clean up the broken pot—"

This time, the interruption came from the far side of the house. "What's all the racket?" Yelled a masculine voice full of gravel and spite from a short staircase, probably an old servants' stair Danita hadn't noticed when she walked into the kitchen. It was behind her, and dark except for the soft glow of in-floor lights on each stair tread. A door at the top of the stairs opened, and a heavy footfall stepped down three steps as the voice muttered, "Damn wolves can't—"

Danita stared at the shadow of a small wide man halted halfway down the stairs.

"You?" said a voice like sand under soft shoes.

Danita blinked as the shadow grew in height. By the time it reached the bottom stair and stepped in front of her, the man stood face-to-face with her. She grasped the golden button on her neck. "It's you," she whispered.

He wore the same loud blue suit and gold striped vest with its shiny gold buttons: the man whose New Year's kiss had shaken her world.

He reached out and took her free hand into his. "Mi querida," he said, but stopped and stared at the button in her other hand. "You're here."

Danita tried but could not gather enough breath to speak.

"You should have called me right away!" Phineas's voice, more like a growl, echoed through the tiny kitchen.

Max's voice called, "Cobalt!"

"I'm sorry," whispered Cobalt. He kissed her fingers. "I'm needed."

Danita nodded. "Yes," was all she could say.

Cobalt pulled himself away from Danita and pushed the swinging door open. "Luna, don't let Bean outside. It's not just a summer storm." Then he walked to the office, muttering under his breath, "Ludicrous lycanthropes. Venomous vampires! The moment something goes wrong, who do they call . . ."

Danita didn't hear what else Cobalt said. The little dog, Bean, trotted to Danita's feet, sat, and stared up at her. "Well," Bean seemed to say to her. "You've picked a dreadful night to stop in."

"Oh, Chihuahua," Danita said, looking down at Bean as though the dog could understand her.

"Where!" shouted Phineas's growl from the back of the house. "Damn it! Tell me where!"

A nervous yap squeaked out of Bean. Danita put her hand to her heart. "Yes, little Chihuahua, a dreadful night." Danita bent down and picked up Bean, who pushed his head into her chest. As Danita scratched his chin, her nerves calmed.

She pushed open the swinging door. Luna stood with the trash bag in one hand and a broom in the other as she stared with wide eyes at the closed door to the office where the men were yelling.

Luna shook her head. In a whispered and shaking voice, she said, "CC and Eugene disappeared."

Danita heard something heavy fall to the floor behind the closed door to CC's office. She wrapped an arm around Luna's shoulders. "Come. When the power comes back on, we'll get the vacuum."

Luna nodded. "When the power is back on—" She stopped and looked at the closed office door.

Cobalt's voice boomed, "No! It'll never work."

"I—I'm not sure what to do," Luna said.

Danita pulled Luna close and hugged her. "They are your good friends. I see that. Be strong and come." The tea kettle whined for attention in the kitchen. "We'll have tea, and we will think."

*****

"Another tornado warning," said Luna, setting her phone back down on the coffee table.

"An enormous storm that's not a summer storm," Danita said.

They sat on the sofa in the living room, lit with two candles. Each sipped hot tea from mismatched coffee mugs and sighed at the latest warnings.

"Gosh," Luna said, taking her feet off the coffee table and sitting up. "I've been so caught up. Is there someone you should call? It's getting late."

"No," said Danita. "I live alone."

Luna returned her feet to the coffee table and leaned back. "My mom's at a conference in Mexico. She's had to delay returning twice because of COVID. I texted my brother. These days, he knows if I say I'm here, I really am. I don't lie to him anymore."

Danita looked into Luna's face, so soft and distant in the candlelight. "Anymore? It's very bad to lie, unless you're helping someone. Then I suppose if it's a good lie it's okay, but it can still kick you in the ass."

Luna laughed. "Don't I know it! Me and Marcus, that's my brother, we used to go at it tooth and claw all the time. These days, we're good. I understand things better now."

"You're still growing up," said Danita, nodding her head. "How old are you?"

"Eighteen. How do you know Cobalt? I didn't know anyone—I mean, I didn't think he had any friends here in town."

Danita put her cup on the coffee table and fanned her face. "It's warm in here."

Luna did a terrible job hiding a grin as she sipped her tea.

Danita burst into laughter. "We can, neither of us, hide our emotions."

Luna put her cup down and joined Danita's laughter.

Danita forced a long sigh. "New Year's Eve, 2019. It was a grand party. I thought 2020 would be a glorious year. I'd just started my new job. Everything looked so good. He gave me a New Year's kiss, and . . ."

Luna leaned forward. "And?"

"It was the most wonderful kiss I've ever had." Danita let her head fall back, and she relived the New Year's kiss from a stranger that changed her life. "This," she pointed to the golden button on its black silk ribbon. "This fell from his vest. I've worn it ever since."

Luna signed. "That's so romantic."

A great howl erupted from the front of the house. Thunder shook the air around them. Wood broke and glass shattered. Both women jumped to their feet.

The swinging door flew open, and Cobalt stood in the doorway, breathing heavy. A trickle of blood dripped from his forehead over his eye. "Luna!" he shouted. "We gotta catch him before he kills somebody."

Luna's lower lip trembled as she breathed in. "Phineas?"

Cobalt wiped his forehead with a handkerchief. "He's pissed. We did all we could, but he'll run all the way to Vegas if we can't stop him. Eugene disappeared with CC when the casino was attacked. Max is already out after him. I gotta help stop him. Fluffy will stay here."

Danita stepped toward Cobalt as she heard Luna whimper, "They've both disappeared?"

Turning back, Danita watched as Luna's shoulders slumped and shook. She took in a deep breath and wrapped her arms around Luna. "I'll stay here with her, my love."

"Thank you," he said. "I thought Phineas was so in control of himself. No matter what you see or hear, don't open the door for anyone, and don't go outside."

Danita nodded.

"Luna," shouted Cobalt.

Luna's pale, sweating face lifted.

"No one, Luna. Promise me you won't open the door for anyone."

Luna nodded.

"She won't," Danita said. "Neither of us will."

*****

Danita put her hand on Luna's cheek. "Luna, we are going to be very brave. Yes?" Danita moved her hand to Luna's chin and lifted the girl's face to look at her. "Yes?"

Luna nodded. "A monster killed my little brother. It tried to kill me too, but I wouldn't let it. I won't let any monster scare me anymore, but . . . Phineas isn't a monster, but he could kill."

Danita stood back as Luna pulled her shoulders back and took in a deep breath. "Luna. Have faith in your friends. They know what they're doing. We will not let someone we can't see frighten us."

Luna nodded. Her mouth tightened into a straight line, and her eyes narrowed. "I'm going to double-check the doors and windows. Cobalt's spells secures them, but let's make sure they're physically locked, too."

"Good idea," Danita said and picked up her phone to turn on the flashlight. "I will follow. Locks are good. Spells are better. And then you must take your exam."

"Danita," Luna said as she rattled the front door before pronouncing it locked. "I have a confession to make."

"Yes," Danita said. "I suspect you do."

Luna sat in her chair at the reception desk. "I don't have an exam tonight."

"Silly girl." Danita smiled and leaned against the large desk. "I told you, we're too much alike. You wear the same face when you lie as I do. Let me guess." She put her finger to her lips. "I bet you want to watch a movie your mother doesn't want you to watch."

Luna's mouth fell open. "That's no fair! How did you know?"

"Your face," Danita said. "It cannot lie. Besides, you forget my position as Secretary to the Director of Communications. I see all memos, and tonight the University servers are down for maintenance."

Luna shook her head, even as her grin widened. "You're good. I better not— Hey! How do you know spells are better?"

The house rattled and a bright white light flashed outside the windows, too bright and too long to be lightning.

"Not lightning," Danita whispered. She listened but heard only her breath and Luna's. Silence slid through her, pressing down on her heart.

"Not thunder," Luna whispered. She jumped to standing and squeezed Danita's arm as someone knocked on the front door.

Luna reached for the keypad on her desk. The monitors would not turn on.

Bright white light flashed again. The windows rattled.

"Luna!" Came a shout from outside the front door. "It's me. Open up, hurry!"

Luna took a step forward, but Danita squeezed her arm and put a finger to her lips, shaking her head. Luna nodded.

"*Mi querida, por fa for*? I've got to get inside," Cobalt yelled, panic edging in his voice.

Danita's hand beat into her chest as tears filled her eyes. Luna looked at her and opened her mouth, but Danita shook her head. She mouthed the words, "We promised."

"Luna!" Cobalt's voice pleaded louder. Desperation echoed through the room. "I can't get Phin to change. Please Luna! He's going to rip me apart."

Danita grabbed both of Luna's shoulders as the girl leaned toward the door. A great howl filled the air outside the house, creeping into the house between the tiny cracks of the walls and windows. Someone screamed.

The front door monitor flickered on, filling the room with a sickly blue light.

On the monitor, Cobalt pounded on the door, his jacket torn down the back, hanging on by threads on his shoulders. Danita watched as his face leaned into the camera. "Hurry! I don't have much time. Luna! Danita! Help me!"

"I can't leave him out there," Luna whispered.

The silence grated on Danita's nerves. Panic filled the face of the man she loved, and still the silence echoed. Too much silence. "Bean," Danita said. She put her face close to Luna's. "Why don't we hear Bean barking? And what about Fluffy?"

Luna looked around. "Bean's a yapping Chihuahua. He should be yapping like mad with someone banging on the door. Fluffy doesn't let anyone in the house unless she wants them in."

Danita, still staring at the monitor, asked, "How tall is Cobalt?"

Luna twisted to look at the monitor. "Shorter than me."

"Not my Cobalt," Danita said. "And look at his vest."

Luna pointed at the figure on the screen. "All his buttons are there. We need a weapon."

Danita looked around her and picked up the broom. "We make do with what we have." She lifted the broom over her head and slammed it on the edge of Luna's desk. It broke in half.

"Luna! Danita!" shouted the not-Cobalt at the door. "Help! Let me in! Hurry!"

Luna reached over the desk and turned the monitor off. The not-Cobalt at the door screamed in pain. The white light stopped flashing and shaking the house. It oozed through crooks and crannies as nausea forced its way into Danita's stomach.

Danita pulled Luna through the swinging door. The living room, with only one window, felt safe. Bean uncurled from his spot on the couch, stretched, and sat up wagging his tail. Fluffy didn't stir from his resting place beneath the coffee table.

"Open the door!" echoed through the house and Danita's bones. The voice no longer pretended to be Cobalt. "Open the door!" The voice growled and spat.

Danita glanced down at Bean and realized he wasn't starting at her or Luna anymore. He stared at the back door, a snarl on his lips and the hair on his back spiking up.

Danita took in a deep breath to enunciate her words. "Luna, the back door. We checked it, right?"

"Sure," Luna said, then stopped to stare. "I keep a key under the step."

The door handle rattled.

"You have a key for the back door, and you leave it outside?" Danita asked.

Luna shrugged her shoulders. "The fancy locks are for show. Besides, Cobalt—"

Bean barked one happy little bark. Danita looked down to see him pacing the couch, tail wagging.

The light outside the window increased in intensity. Danita and Luna both lifted their arms to shield their eyes. The wind roared, and the back door flew off its hinges into the small stove. At the same moment, darkness surrounded them.

Danita gripped her stick in front of her, ready to charge, even as she and Luna wrapped arms around each other. Cold, icy fingers tickled Danita's spine. Her breath caught as cold seeped through her. Even the warmth of Luna's body next to her faltered.

"No!" Danita shouted, unsure where the words or the strength came from. She pushed Luna behind her, wrapped her free hand around the button on her neck. Pointing her stick where the door should be, she shouted, "You're not invited here. Go away!"

Despite the enveloping darkness, Danita saw a shadow rise only feet away from them. Heat crawled out of her hand, up her arm, into her core. Luna must have felt it, too, as she gasped, tightening her grip on Danita's shoulder. The stick in her hand glowed gold and blue. And then a great roar like dread and death kissing erupted around them, and paws pushed her to the floor.

Danita's head hit the corner of the coffee table. Stars filled her eyes, but before blackness clouded her wits, a figure grew next to the shadow. White fur ruffled and grew long. A paw, then a hand, white and thin like death, gripped the shadow. A face with a long nose and a blue eye burning like a gem in flames formed words in a voice familiar but distant, so soft, so angry, so compelling.

"No one enters this house without my blessing. Remember me, and tell them this from Midnight: You bring your war to my house, I end it. We don't run away."

That's all Danita heard.

*****

"Danita." A voice called to her from far away. She lay in fresh green grass under a bright yellow sun. The smell of mamma's *hojaldre* frying with eggs and sausages drifted in the air.

"Danita, you need to wake up," her mother said. But it wasn't her mother's voice.

Opening her eyes, she looked at a strange ceiling and the face of a Chihuahua licking her face. "*Estoy despierta*," she muttered as she sat up. Her hand went to her head as pain shot through her brain. The little dog curled into her lap.

Video of downed trees and flooded streets under sunny skies flashed across the enormous television screen. Danita pushed aside a blanket and the dog as she put her feet on the floor.

"Morning," Luna said, walking in front of the television screen. Her smile filled her face. Her eyes were bright as she bit into a thick piece of fried bread. "Max made breakfast before he left. Everything's hot, and I made coffee. That's something else I learned to do well while working at the family coffee shop. Want some?"

Danita shook her head. "What time is it?"

"Almost seven," Luna answered.

"I have to get ready for work," Danita said. She tottered as she stood, but with a slow breath, her feet remained firm on the floor.

Luna laughed. "It's Saturday. You can go back to sleep if you like. With the roads like they are, you're not going to get anywhere fast, anyway. I'd have let you sleep longer, but Max said I should wake you every hour until you could stand on your own."

Danita put her hand on her hips. "Thank you, Luna, but—" The smell of the *hojaldre*, eggs, sausage, and cheese filled her nose. Her mouth watered, and her stomach growled. She turned and faced the kitchen. "It smells so good."

"Max is a great cook—I mean chef. He's always reminding me he's a chef not a cook. He knows what he's doing in the kitchen," Luna said between bites of food. "He's the chef at the family coffee shop. Turned the shop around when he bought into it. He said he hopes you like the *hojaldre*, it's been a long time since he made them."

Danita touched her head. "Ow."

"Careful," Luna said. "You got a big bump on your head when Cobalt pushed us out of the way."

"Cobalt?"

Luna nodded her head until she swallowed. "You called him with the button. Somehow or another, he used Fluffy to send that thing away."

Danita closed her eyes, seeing the shadow in the darkness growing before her, seeing the other figure. Not seeing Cobalt with his hand on the thing's neck, lifting it. When she opened her eyes, sunlight streamed through the small window. Sighing, she removed the cloche on the kitchen island, revealing the food. Keeping her head down, she placed food on a plate. "Where is he?"

"Cobalt?" Luna asked.

"Yes - and your friend, Phineas? Is he well?" Danita poured coffee into a cup.

A long sigh escaped Luna's lips. She sat on the edge of the chair next to the sofa where Danita sat, placing her plate on the coffee table. "They stopped him. I think he would have run all the way to Vegas if they hadn't. As it is, he's driving. He wouldn't wait for anyone else. He's so worried about Eugene. There's trouble—" Her eyes watered.

Danita sipped her coffee and then reached out to put her hand on Luna's. "I'm sorry. They must be good friends for you to worry so."

Luna nodded. Her lips were tight, and she stared at the plate of food on her coffee table. Danita said nothing, waiting for Luna to say what she now debated telling her.

"Danita," Luna said. "Max said I should trust you with the truth. Cobalt said you'd understand—that you already know he's not human. He'd come down and tell you himself, but something about rules. Anyway, he's in the attic."

"Yes?" Danita asked.

Luna's eyebrows knitted and her lips straightened. "That thing last night, that broke the door down. Cobalt said it was kind of like a shadow of someone far away from here. Whoever it was couldn't actually be here, so he sent his shadow instead. Does that make sense?"

The image of the white hand on the throat of the shadow, the memory of Cobalt's voice like boulders rolling down a mountain from the face of the dog, flooded Danita's mind again. A shiver ran up her spine. "The shadow was solid. It pushed in the door."

"That won't happen again," Luna nodded. "Cobalt's made sure of that." Luna's shoulders shook. She shuddered and her eyes stared at the boarded up back door. "Max says we have to be careful. They'll try again."

Danita rubbed the golden button around her neck. The fear they'd shared last night bound her to this young woman. "When I was a little girl, I had a friend who lived in the cocoa trees of my father's plantation, a *Dunedes*. Grandmother knew he was there. We played games, and he told me stories. I never doubted he told me the truth. He told me I was touched, like my grandmother was. We both can see those who don't want to be seen by ordinary humans."

"Like CC," said Luna. She poured more coffee into their cups. "Who-ever it was attacked the house last night knows who we are, both of us."

"Yes," Danita said. "If I hadn't kissed Cobalt on New Year's Eve . . ."

"He shouldn't have kissed you," Luna retorted with a snarl. "He knows better."

Danita shook her head. Her lips turned up as the memory of the kiss returned. "No. My heart says we would do it again." She shook her head and pulled her shoulders back. "How are you," she added, waving her hand in the air, "connected to all of this?"

Luna shrugged. "For one, I've been around them—unhumans, it's what they call themselves—so much I can spot most of them now, even when they think they're being careful not to be noticed."

Danita nodded. "Goblins and?"

Luna sat up. "Max is a vampire. He thinks I might become a vamp one day. CC says I wouldn't make a very good one, and she would know. I mean, she can see souls, or something like that. Like you, I think. Phineas is a werewolf. It all sounds too weird, doesn't it? Not sure how I feel about becoming a vampire."

Danita nodded. "I knew what Cobalt was after the kiss." She continued to rub the button on her neck.

Luna patted Danita's shoulder. "Cobalt will come down tonight to see you, if you're here."

Danita lowered her head, knowing her cheeks burned. "Yes?"

"He's not leaving the house again." Luna stood and took her plate to the kitchen. "We're the good guys, Danita. I promise, but the way you look when you think about Cobalt tells me you already know that. Can't believe how hungry I am." Luna filled her plate with more food. "You were so brave last night. Me, I could hardly move, but you were all like, 'Don't mess with me!' And like ready to run that shadow through with that wooden stick. Max said that would've worked, too. Not that it was a vamp. I mean, like what could live with a wooden handle sticking in it? You saved the day. Everybody can spend their time helping get CC and Eugene get back, thanks to you. Want more to eat? There's plenty."

Danita shuddered. Looking up, she saw Luna staring at her. "We make a good team, Luna. I too am very hungry."

L.K. Latham writes Urban Fantasy and poetry that's about as dark as the chocolate she loves. She fills her days writing about vampires, werewolves, and other creatures of the shadows. A Texas native, L.K. enjoys the company of the wines of Texas a bit more than some of its inhabitants, but that doesn't stop her from admiring their spunk and veracity in the face of overwhelming facts.

Now living in Austin, Texas, L.K. claims teaching, technical writing, and training as former professions. They are, however, tucked away, only recurring in the occasional nightmare. She enjoys cooking something chocolate as she waits for last year's grapes to become this year's wine.